ABOUT JENNI JAMES

### Reviews for Pride & Popularity
### (The Jane Austen Diaries) :

"This book was unputdownable. I highly
recommend it to any fan of Jane Austen,
young or old. Impatiently awaiting the rest of
the series."

—*Jenny Ellis, Librarian and Jane Austen*
*Society of North America*

"Having read several other Young Adult
retellings of Pride and Prejudice - I must admit
that Pride and Popularity by Jenni James
is my top choice and receives my highest
recommendation! In my opinion, it is the most
plausible, accessible, and well-crafted YA
version of Pride and Prejudice I have read! I
can hardly wait to read the [next] installment
in this series!"

—*Meredith, Austenesque Reviews*

"I started reading Pride and Popularity and
couldn't put it down! I stayed up until 1:30 in
the morning to finish. I've never been happier
to lose sleep. I was still happy this morning.
You can't help but be happy when reading this

feel good book. Thank you Jenni for the fun night!"

—Clean Teen Fiction

### Reviews for Northanger Alibi (The Jane Austen Diaries):

"Twilight obsessed teens (and their moms) will relate to Claire's longing for the fantastical but will be surprised when they find the hero is even better than a vampire or werewolf. Hilarious, fun and romantic!"

—TwilightMOMS.com

"Stephenie Meyer meets Jane Austen in this humorous, romantic tale of a girl on a mission to find her very own Edward Cullen. I didn't want it to end!"

—Mandy Hubbard, author of Prada & Prejudice

"We often speak of Jane Austen's satiric wit, her social commentary, her invention of the domestic novel. But Jenni James, in this delicious retelling of Northanger Abbey, casts new light on Austen's genius in portraying relationships and the foibles of human nature--in this case, the projection of our literary fantasies onto our daily experience."

—*M.M. Bennetts, author of May 1812.*

## Reviews for Prince Tennyson:

"After reading Prince Tennyson, your heart will be warmed, tears will be shed, and loved ones will be more appreciated. Jenni James has written a story that will make you believe in miracles and tender mercies from above."
—*Sheila Staley, Book Reviewer & Writer*

"Divinely inspired, beautifully written—a must read!"
—*Gerald D. Benally, author of Premonition (2013)*

"Prince Tennyson is a sweet story that will put tears in your eyes and hope in your heart at the same time."
—*Author Shanti Krishnamurty*

# Chapter One

"ARRRRUUUGHHHHHH!"

The prince half sobbed, half howled into the night air—his feeble skin ripped, agonizingly making way for the tormented form to escape. Nearly doubled over, he'd never known such excruciating pain before, and yet the old woman continued to laugh at him.

Her unmerciful cackles pierced his ears louder than his tearing skin.

Sickened and dazed, the transformation ended with a jolt, leaving a deep-rooted throbbing ache throughout his whole form. Everything stung with the awareness of newly stretched and swollen limbs. Taking a ginger step, he practically fell over from the searing nerve endings as they shot up from the soles of his feet to his legs and back. Tender, singed and unprotected newness covered his whole form. He was so preoccupied with trying to cope, he didn't hear the woman until she repeated herself.

"You'll be sore for quite some time, so you'd better get used to it." Her laughter grated again.

"Why?" gasped the prince, "Why me? Why now?" He tried to straighten and turn to meet her gaze more fully, but while attempting to, he stumbled and collapsed. Fire surged through every bone as his raw nerves met the harsh ground. The pain was more unbearable than the transformation. Nausea flooded into his pounding skull and threatened to spew out his throat onto the ground if he didn't hold as still as possible.

He felt her cane grind into his hip, but he was too weak to acknowledge it.

"You, boy, needed to be taught a lesson." She jabbed the sharp stick and continued, "Now you will forever know what it feels like to be ugly. Your eyes are too hazy at the moment to even see the figure you've become, but when you awaken"—she moved the cane to his inflamed disjointed knee and dug deep into the taut tissue. He flinched and writhed in agony, his howls filling the darkened forest—"and you will awaken. You may wish you were dead, but however, that is not the purpose of such a transformation. You will live through this—it will be several days until you're healed enough to make it back to your castle, Prince." She hissed his title as if it were the curse and not her hex. "At that point, when you're able to crawl up the stately stairs to your fine room, I want you to haul yourself up upon your chiseled table and peer into the looking glass. Take in every inch of your demented form.

"That will be the day you embrace what has truly happened to you and the day you realize what it means to be a hideous beast forever."

"NO!" he yelped as her cane lashed at his engorged, twisted spine. "Please…" His body convoluted. Nausea swam in dizzying circles until he could no longer focus on anything but the bile rising, aching to relieve itself, as the cane pounded again and again.

The old woman wheezed and thankfully the whacking stopped. She coughed for some time before weakly sputtering out the rest of the curse. "Y-you will be forced to stay this way forever, half man, half beast—unless you find some poor, pitiful female to embrace, accept, and love you for the monster that you are."

Her breathing became more labored. "You h-have one year to achieve that impossible feat. O-one year from today to ch-change your spoilt habits and become a man. If-if you do not succeed, you will be forced to roam the earth in your gruesome form, terrorizing all who meet you, c-causing them to flee in fear from your presence. Though I must warn you—"

She wheezed again, a huge snarled inhale, which forced a series of bone-rattling hacks from her. They became larger and more pronounced with each cough—precious air forcing its way into her battered lungs.

The prince felt the space around him shift, before he heard the thud of her collapse and the silence that followed.

It was several minutes before he was able to slowly scrape his body against the earth in painful strides enough to see her, and another several minutes before he could move his limbs enough to ascertain that she was indeed dead.

He smiled then, a bitter hate-filled smile.

CECELIA'S EYES FLUTTERED open and she stretched and arched to the glorious sunshine trickling through her window. The day was warm and welcoming—her toes wiggled in excitement under the delicate patchwork quilt her grandmother had especially designed for her. Today was the day she was going to cast off being Miss Cecelia Hammerstein-Smythe, and instead become the girl promised to Lord Charles David Willington, the most perfect man in existence.

She squealed a very unladylike squeal and hopped from the bed, her black braid bobbing and swaying with her. Within minutes she'd washed in the hand basin and without waiting for her maid, dressed in a pretty white morning

frock with a lavender sash and adornments.
Whirling around like a little girl she watched
the dress fan out below her stockings and
smiled.

The world was a wonderful place. And
she, Miss Hammerstein-Smythe, was very
grateful indeed to be a part of it.

With a delightful curtsy to no one in
particular and jaunty half minuet step, she
made her way to the wardrobe, dipped inside
fetching her lavender slippers and placed
them quickly upon her very happy feet before
tripping lightly down the stairs into her
mother's breakfast parlor to greet Sanford's
impassive countenance.

"Good morning to you too!" she trilled out
lightly as she skipped past the butler into the
waiting room. "Cook has outdone herself this
morning, has she not?" Cecelia giggled. It
had to have been for her. The platters loaded
on the sideboard were all of her most favorite
breakfast foods. And when she turned she
saw a huge bowl upon the middle of the table.
"Look at that fruit! How could I ever eat half
as much food?"

"Well, you know how Mrs. Parnel dotes

on you. We're all fortunate enough she hadn't the time to go shopping—or we'd be looking at twice as much food." The butler grinned at his mild humor, before schooling his features into a more appropriate look and announcing rather grandly, "I have received word from Jenkins that we are to expect your special visitor around two this afternoon, where he would like to take you driving in his carriage, if you are so inclined?"

Cecelia's eyes sparkled over her plate she was filling from the sideboard. "I am very much inclined, as you well know."

"I will be sure to see your reply of acceptance is sent immediately. Sanford poured her a cup of tea and set it upon the saucer on the table while a young footman held a chair for her and pushed it in as she sat down.

It only took a few minutes of eating and another half hour or so of deciding on the very best outfit to be seen in the open carriage with Lord Willington. After she saw that her maid laid the dress out to be worn later, Cecelia quickly grabbed her pelisse, buttoned it over her white and lavender morning gown and made her way outside before her mother or William, her stuffy older brother, could persuade her otherwise. She was just tying the bow to her bonnet at a rakish angle as she entered the pathway that led to the cheerful brook not quite a mile from the great house.

She loved the water, and anytime she needed a quick break from life, she would find herself sneaking off to enjoy a cool moment of refreshing solitude where no one could bother her.

Once she'd made it to the brook, it was no time at all before her slippers and stockings were off and stuffed safely into the crook of a tree branch. Her bonnet and pelisse were soon to follow, hanging rather precariously from the stub just below her shoes.

With a sigh, Cecelia sank onto her favorite rock and carelessly trailed her bare feet and ankles in the water. She made sure her gown was tucked away from the water's edge, or there would be no explaining the scolding she would receive from her mother for ruining yet another frock.

She took a deep breath and leaned back against the large stone, enjoying the peaceful smell of grass and wildflowers, her ears rejoicing over the soft babble of the little stream beneath her. This was exactly what a perfect day should be. There was no need for anything more enjoyable than such perfection. In fact, she was positive, with the soon-to-be proposal from Lord Willington and the glorious peace-filled morning before her, there had never been a more perfect day during the whole of her existence.

And nothing, absolutely nothing, could ruin it.

Prince Alexander halted in his tracks at the lovely girl before him. He could just make out her profile with her back to the rock like that. Her hair was in wild abandon, with its long curls escaping the bun that was now quite forgotten and rather disheveled looking. His eyes skimmed past her pert nose down her sweet lips, then on to the hand that was softly skimming over the grass beneath it. Her legs moved then and he quickly looked away when he noticed they were uncovered.

His heart began to beat fast.

What if he were caught?

Prince Alexander knew it would be highly uncomfortable to them both, she in her state of undress and he the chosen prince of the land escaping his castle. He had been roaming farther and wider from the palace than normal of late. Escaping the confines of the huge monstrous place, he needed to be outdoors. He needed to see where it was his demented form took him to each evening. Just last night, transformed into the beast, he'd come across this exact brook and had been eager to see what it looked like in the daylight. He came as soon as he'd awoken from his night's adventures and had become his usual self again. What had seemed like a good idea earlier, now all of the sudden seemed very bad indeed.

## Chapter Two

WHY MUST HE make so much noise? A few moments ago, Alexander barely heard the crunching his boots made as he'd rushed along the wooded trail. Now, it would seem every step he took echoed across the whole land. Gingerly he took another pace backward, the leaves and forest floor covering snapping beneath his weight. He prayed the sound of the water and her own thoughts would distract the girl enough to allow him his escape.

Another couple of steps and he would be out of her eyesight at least, though he'd have to keep quiet a bit longer than that. Who knew how sharp her ears were.

Alexander could almost taste his freedom, when just then he startled a small rabbit from its hiding spot under the bush to his right. The animal scurried loudly across the forest floor and headed straight for the girl.

She glanced up at the sudden movement and caught the prince as he was ready to flee himself. Her eyes grew wide with shock and the inevitable anger quickly replaced her beautiful looks into the scowling fortress before him.

He mumbled under his breath, not realizing until it was too late, exactly who he had disrupted. Her face had been hidden just enough to not recognize her until now. It would have been his luck to stumble across the only female in the land who absolutely loathed him and had no problem telling him so to his face whenever she had the opportunity. How did the fates find him this fortunate? What were the odds of such an occurrence, really?

"You?!"

Miss Hammerstein-Smythe's outraged shriek he was certain could be heard for miles.

Already Alexander's hands were up in a defensive gesture. "Now, wait a moment.

This is not what it looks like. I merely—"

"You have been following me! I knew it." She quickly scrambled to her feet and brushed her gown down over her bare legs. "How long have you been spying on me?"

"I wasn't. I was simply on my way to the brook having no idea you would be here."

Cecelia placed her hands on her hips and faced him. "You expect me to believe you, Prince Alexander, decided to simply wander all the way from your castle to my father's property, to my exact favorite spot along this whole streambed, where you could've stopped anywhere, at the exact same time I would be here, and that it was not because of me?"

"No. Yes! I do expect you to believe just that, because it is the truth."

"What do you want from me? Why must every time I search for peace I find you?"

"I'm sure it's not every time." He watched her arch an eyebrow. "Look, nothing. Nothing. I want nothing. I don't even want to talk to you."

She scrunched her nose slightly and tilted her head. "Why should I believe you?"

Alexander moved forward just a step.

"Because, as I said, it is the truth."

Cecelia was embarrassed, completely mortified if she were honest, but she would die before she let the prince know how upsetting his presence was. Instead, she did what she always did in such confrontations and went on the attack. "I do not believe you." She took a step forward and then paused when she felt her foot crunch on the prickly forest floor. "You have never before told the truth—always bragging and lying about anything and everything—why should I care to listen to what you say now?" She folded her arms very unladylike and continued, "As far as I'm concerned you came here to torment me, so out with it." She defiantly lifted her chin in an obvious challenge. "Say whatever lies and bullying you'd like, we're on even ground now, you and I, with you on my father's property and so far away from your palace guards. Tell me."

The prince shook his head. "Miss Hammerstein-Smythe I'm not here to quarrel with you again. You can keep your solitude. Forgive me for the interruption, I wish you a good day." With that he quickly bowed at the waist and turned on his heel to make a hasty retreat. He didn't care where he went as long as it was as far away from the girl as he could get.

"Wait." Cecelia cursed her impulse to call him back so quickly, but the damage had been done.

Alexander paused, but did not turn fully around. "Yes?"

Nervously she clutched the sides of her gown. "I—you, what is wrong?"

He turned toward her. "Wrong?"

Goodness, would she never learn to keep her mouth shut? She took another step forward, heedless of the sharp floor below, she felt compelled to continue. "There's something different about you. What is it?"

Alexander attempted a laugh. To his chagrin, it came out sounding more like a nervous goat bleating, which he quickly covered with a cough. "There's nothing wrong with me. Nothing different at all. What do you mean?"

She grinned. She couldn't help it. He looked just like the neighbor's son when he was caught snitching Cook's pastries. "Where

are my insults? Have you nothing rude to
say to me? You've never stopped before
from saying exactly what was on your mind.
Why is today an exception? Something has
happened."

Could she tell? Was he really different?
The prince half-heartedly replied, "I can have
you hanged for treason if you keep this up."

Cecelia laughed right out loud. "That's
the best you can do? Now I know something
is wrong! What is it?"

There was nothing that annoyed him more
than meddling nosy females, and she was the
absolute worst at interfering. Always poking
and prying herself into everyone's business.
He'd seen her countless times querying and
discussing all sorts of things with anyone she
was around. Helping herself to offer advice,
counsel, and even ailment curing to anyone
from the maid to the people of the court. It
was bad enough to think she thought he was
different, it was quite another to subject
oneself to her pitying and snooping. Before
he'd know it, she'd be finding all sorts of
things "wrong" with him and trying to poke
and pry into his life like she did everyone else.

"Excuse me, Miss. I will leave you to your own imaginings on what you believe to be flawed with me." With that he bowed again and left. Not caring if he ever saw Miss Cecelia Hammerstein-Smythe again. In fact, he was positive if he never saw her again, it would be too soon.

CECELIA QUICKLY FORGOT about the prince as she came back toward the house an hour or so later. She'd thought about him enough as it was that afternoon, with his strange behavior and abrupt departure. But now was not the time to worry over him, now was the time to begin her preparations for the wonderful Lord Willington. In no time at all she'd bathed, powdered, dressed, and primped for the delightful man, until she was simply the beauty of perfection in emerald green stripes. Her long curls artfully arranged by her maid in a sumptuous updo, purposefully designed to capture the heart of all who looked upon her. Or more importantly to secure the heart of one who was already hers.

She giggled as she turned from side to side

at precisely a quarter past the hour and knew then she'd never seen herself look so happy or so fine. In just a few moments everything would change in her life—simply everything. And she could not wait!

Cecelia elegantly made her way down the wide staircase, slowing her steps to appear much more refined than she felt at the moment. Her purposeful approach a few minutes late also had the same effect. One should never try to appear too eager, or it gives the courter an unfair advantage over you.

"Miss Hammerstein-Smythe, you look ravishing!"

Lord Willington bowed, his shiny blond locks bobbed a bit, causing her heart to flutter to a stop. Cecelia loved the way Charles' curls broke free from their confined hair treatments once his hat was off. She loved every aspect of him, but she did not let it show beyond a glimmer in her eyes as she curtsied. "Thank you. You look very fine, as well."

She stepped into the pelisse the maid held out for her, and allowed the young girl to button the pretty overcoat, while she slipped her hands into her short white gloves.

A moment later her matching bonnet was perched atop her head and she was ready to go. Beaming, Cecelia turned toward Lord Willington's waiting arm, gratefully clutched it, and with a quick farewell to Sanford they were walking out into the glorious sunshine. She was gallantly handed in the carriage by Lord Willington himself, causing the rapid beating of her heart to become so loud she wondered if he could hear it.

In a trice they were off, and the clop, clop, clop of the horses' sprightly hooves did much to increase her excitement. Many people came to their windows to watch them leave. They had quite become the talk of the village, and soon, very soon, they would be all celebrating with her at the grand engagement ball her mother and brother had been spreading word about.

Yes, life was joyously splendid.

After a few minutes at a very brisk trot winding through the village and countryside, Lord Willington pulled the carriage to a little alcove, nearly completely hidden within the copse of trees and low lying branches. It was there, with the reins in his hands, he finally

turned and looked fully at the handsome girl
beside him.

Charles had never seen anyone more
beautiful than Cecelia. He allowed his eyes to
wander lovingly across her delicate features
and paused to contemplate her most perfectly
delectable rose-colored lips. Nothing had
been more tempting to him than kissing
her, but it would not do. Not today, not the
day when he'd purposely set out to tell her
of his Kathryn, his Lady Dashenwold, his
intended from Baythorpe Hall. No, he needed
everything as perfect as it could be to break
the news as gently as possible to her. For there
was no way he'd ever be allowed to wed this
beautiful creature next to him. Not without
the proper lineage behind her. Not without the
proper fortune to satisfy his father. Yes, she
had a large home and her family had obviously
been wealthy enough for the village, but not
enough to please his father. He wanted his
dear son to make an excellent match, to an
excellent lineage with excellent connections.
No, indeed, Miss Cecelia Hammerstein-
Smythe would never be the proper wife
for Lord Willington and he hoped against

hope she'd already come to this exact same conclusion.

## Chapter Three

"WELL, OF COURSE, I never thought any such thing! My goodness, imagine me thinking I would marry you!" Cecelia exclaimed with a forced smile upon her face, which she prayed looked real. "You deserve as much happiness as anyone. And Lady Dashenwold sounds the exact person to bring you such happiness."

Cecelia had no idea what she was saying. The lies escaped so easily from her tongue she wondered briefly if the prince had rubbed off on her.

Her hands were still clasped within Lord Willington's strong hold. She didn't want to let go. She knew she'd never be able to hold his hands in such a way again. But, she didn't want to hold on either. She couldn't. They weren't her hands to hold.

"And when did you propose to her?" Her fingers tightened upon his, showing the only sign of how painful such a question was to ask. She hoped he mistook the unconscious action as a sign of eagerness. Laughing gaily she remarked, "I wish I could have been there to witness it. Was it as truly romantic as any girl could hope for?"

Cecelia could not hear the words he spoke; it was as if her own ears were protecting her from such vileness. All she could make out was the dreaded pounding of her heart and voice inside her head repeatedly telling her to leave. Run. Quick, before he caught her crying over him.

How did she ever find herself in such a predicament? Whatever would she tell her mother and her brother, William? They would never let her live this down. Ever. She would become the complete laughingstock of the whole village. And yet, she could not keep this charade up. She must tell them. They must know Charles never meant to propose to her at all and, in fact, was very much, at this moment, decidedly engaged to another.

How she kept her composure the whole way home was a miracle unto itself, and one she could not completely identify as having anything to do with. She was in a state of utter shock. She was not coherent, she had no recollection of anything she had said or was saying. But by the good graces of luck, she'd found herself answering, giggling and doing all things happy and proper. It was as if her body were on some sort of automatic reaction and the real Cecelia Hammerstein-Smythe was very far away looking down upon it all in a sad reminiscence of everything she believed she once had and saying goodbye to a world that would now never be hers.

She was shattered. She was heartbroken beyond anything she'd ever known before.

Oh, how she had loved him. How she did love him still! There was nothing she would not have done for him, nothing she would not have given him. And yet, it still was not enough. He did not want her.

He wanted another.

In a grateful haze, Cecelia thanked Lord
Willington and made her way up the stairs to
her room. One look at the butler as she passed
was enough to let him see she needed a few
hours of privacy. Sanford would take care
of everything for her and make her excuses
until she could face them all. Plopping onto
her bed, she took enough time to remove her
pelisse and bonnet, setting them on the bench
in front of the footboard, before curling up in a
ball—driving boots and all—and burying her
face into her pillow.

Several hours later, Cecelia opened her
eyes to a darkened room. She was still in her
gown, but it looked as though her maid had
come in and sweetly placed a blanket over
her. Rolling on her back, she could just make
out the moon as it slivered through the cracks
of the curtains. It was quite high, signifying
the night was well underway. Blinking and
stretching a bit, she debated over removing
her shoes and putting on her nightgown or
just staying as she was. But she wasn't tired.
And now that she was awake, memories of
that afternoon came flooding back with a
vengeance.

Groaning, she flew the cover off of her and sat up. This would never do. She simply could not waste another moment of her life sniveling over Lord Willington. Cecelia hopped down from the bed and paced around the room, acting more like a caged lion than a girl deep in thought.

She needed out. She needed air. Room to breathe. A change of environment. Peace. Something.

Halting to a stop, she reached over and grabbed her pelisse and bonnet from the small bench. Before she'd completely rationalized all that she was doing, she'd donned them both and threw the small blanket over her like a shawl for added warmth. Then as quickly and as silently as possible, she made her way down the servants' staircase and out the back door to freedom.

The brook. She needed to get to her brook. It was the only thing that would calm her now. And she needed it more than she needed anything else in her life.

Her mother would kill her if she knew the danger she was placing herself in, but honestly, what could be out there? Everyone else was asleep. The only real danger she faced was the few night animals roaming the forest. But she was larger and scarier than any of them could be to her. The moon was high enough to light her path so she wouldn't get lost. Besides, she could probably walk the whole trail to the little stream completely blindfolded she knew the way so well.

She was completely safe. More safe here than with her thoughts.

PRINCE ALEXANDER SHUDDERED at the transformation as he ran beyond the castle grounds, still not used to the agonizing pain of his skin tearing to make way for the wolf within him. Even though it had been about four months since he'd first been cursed by the witch, each night he relived the horror all over again. He'd hoped by now he would've become more used to the sensation, but alas, pain, pain, and more pain was all he ever knew.

Tonight was more agonizing than the rest, and to add to it time was running out. From what he could gather, he needed to find a girl

to love him as an ugly wolf before the year
was over, or he'd remain a beast forever. It
seemed a hopeless cause. The witch was right;
he was a monster, inside and out.

He didn't always feel that way. After the
first few weeks, every time he thought of the
old woman he'd wanted to kill her all over
again. How he hated her. But now, now it'd
been so long, he'd begun to see things in a
different light. For a prince, he wasn't the
best, and his kingdom suffered greatly for it.
They needed a better ruler than some selfish
brat to take over the throne when his mother
died. They needed a strong, valiant man who
loved them. His father, when he was alive,
had been one of the best kings this country
had ever had. It was not fair to either of his
parents to have a son so determined to have his
own way and destined to disgrace them both.

Since the transformation had begun, there
were many nights where Alexander had tried
to destroy himself. Thinking death was the
answer, he was positive nothing could be
worse than his fate. How wrong he was. Now
he knew differently. Now he knew just how
needed he was. And he hoped he had enough

time to makes things right for his family, before his dreadful secret was out. He simply could not rule as a beast, but he'd hoped to help his cousin see the great responsibility and prepare him to take over the throne. There was less than eight months before no one would ever be able to see him again.

She was right, that girl—Miss Hammerstein-Smythe—he was different. He was very different. But it was too late.

Perhaps it was because he was thinking of her, perhaps it was because he really needed some solitude tonight, or perhaps it was because the place seemed magical, whatever the reason, Alexander found himself, as a wolf, at the same place he'd discovered the night before—the gentle brook.

Except this time he was not alone.

She had been weeping for quite some time. He was certain of it. In fact, he'd never seen the gel so at a loss before in his life. If someone were to ask him if she ever cried, he would not have hesitated to respond in the negative. Yet, here Miss Hammerstein-Smythe was crying as if her world had ended.

Did she often come to this place and cry in

secret? She seemed so peaceful earlier today. Had something happened?

A surge of sympathy shot through him as he crept forward on silent paws to see if he could be of some comfort for her. He was just about to announce his presence when it dawned on him he might very well frighten her in his present form.

CECELIA FELT THE hairs on the back of her neck rise. They were quickly followed by gooseflesh erupting all over her back and arms.

She was not alone.

Her ears picked up the gentle sound of the water trickling, as well as the midnight breeze rustling through the forest trees—nothing to alarm her. Yet, still the feeling she was being watched would not go away.

Cecelia wiped away a few tears with her left hand to distract her would-be assailant while surreptitiously gripping the thick branch lying just under her gown and out of sight. She'd collected it on the way down just in case a situation like this did arise. Her father had always reminded her to be vigilant and aware of everything around her. And after today's earlier scare with the prince she wasn't about to take any chances.

With her hand clutching the large branch, she slowly raised her head and took in all of her surroundings at once. Her eyes scanned the dark crooks and crevices of the trees around her. Whatever, whoever was out there, was right behind her. It was as if she could almost hear their breathing if only she listened more intently.

Cecelia's father had always warned about danger and men who might try to assault her. She learned early in life the best time to fight off an attack was to do so immediately while the enemy was still catching their bearings and not fully certain of their plan. She had to be swift, strong and urgent in defending herself to guarantee they would flee or leave her alone long enough that she could get to safety.

If she wanted to catch them off guard, it was now or never.

Heaving herself from the ground in one rapid movement, she spun around, hurling her thick branch forward and forcing the wind from her throat in a loud guttural howl.

# Chapter Four

THE LARGE BRANCH connected with its target perfectly.

In fact, Cecelia would've never believed her aim was so good if she hadn't seen it with her own eyes. Watching the great animal flinch and drop before her was unbelievable! She'd actually struck the poor thing right upon its forehead. Who knew she had it in her? If only William could've been there to witness it. He'd never believe her now.

Her crowing and general self congratulations did not last too long though, for almost immediately the wolf began to moan and move about.

She grabbed the branch from where it had ricocheted after striking the animal, ready to flee or attack if she had to.

She didn't have to.

For in that moment, the beast's groans began to take on a different sound altogether. They were almost human-like and it was several seconds before Cecelia realized he was actually speaking to her!

"I'm sorry. Did you say something to me?" she asked, still unsure if she was imagining more than she was willing to admit.

"Yes," he grunted.

Cecelia quickly crouched for the attack. "Did you just say, 'Yes'?"

"Of course, I did."

Stunned, she could not help asking, "Did you just say, 'Of course, I'—?"

"Yes! Look." The beast rolled over onto his hind legs and gingerly sat up as he spoke. "I know this may be a novel concept for you, but, yes, I'm speaking and, yes, you can hear me."

Stepping back, she stumbled over a small boulder next to the water and caught herself just in time. "I-I don't believe it."

"Well, it's the truth." He stretched his paws and leaned back a bit, with a look of submission, so as not to alarm her more. "I'm not sure what else I should do to convince you otherwise, except speak. Though considering your reaction, I feel it may not be the best way."

Cecelia slowly lowered herself to the rock, the green striped gown gracefully puddling around her. "But how?"

"How can I talk?" Alexander wasn't quite sure what answer he should give that wouldn't reveal his secret, so he evaded the question instead by rubbing his head against his front legs. "Well, it was much easier to communicate coherently before I was clubbed to death."

A surprised chuckle escaped her lips. "It was a branch, barely a stick, and it only hit you once."

"With quite some force, let me tell you."

"Yes, well, what did you expect sneaking up behind me like that?"

Alexander grumbled, "I didn't suppose you to be so acute, certainly." He rubbed his head on his front legs trying to receive a tad bit more sympathy from Miss Hammerstein-Smythe. "Nor did I imagine your aim to be quite so faultless either."

Sympathy did not come from Cecelia's corner, she was too ecstatic and bewildered by the night's events to fully comprehend what was happening, or remember her manners. "I know! I could not believe it myself! And then to watch you fall like that was mind-boggling."

The wolf did not miss the excited glimmer in her eyes, or the fact that he'd never seen the girl look prettier. "Or mind-bashing," he moaned in response, before lying his stomach fully upon the ground. "Either way you'd like to look at it, it hurt."

"Did it hurt very much then?" She leaned forward, placing her elbows on her knees. "It looked like it was extremely painful."

Alexander's deep rumbling chuckle was foreign to his ears. He wasn't sure when the last time was he had actually laughed out loud, but he was positive he'd never had the opportunity as a beast. "Honestly, I'd be more eager to answer that question if I thought you were asking out of sympathy and not crooning delight."

Cecelia laughed with him. "I'm sorry. I should be more empathetic, should I not?"

"Definitely."

She arched an eyebrow and grinned while coyly smoothing down her dress. "Yes, but how do I know all of this isn't just a ploy to catch me off my guard so you can strike?"

If Alexander could have rolled his eyes he would have, instead he settled with a pathetic sigh and lowered his head to his paws. "Believe me, my dear Miss Hammerstein-Smythe, had I wanted to kill you I'd have done it way before you became aware of my presence."

Her smile fell, and her face paled even greater within the ghastly glow of the moonlight. "Who are you?"

"What?" He raised his head, titling it to the side. He could smell fear in the air. "What's wrong? What have I said?"

"How do you know my name?" Her skirts rustled as she stood up and began to inch away again, her fist tightly clutching the branch. "Who are you?"

He would've cursed out loud if he hadn't

been in front of a female. "I'm not here to harm you. I was thirsty and needed a respite when I came across a beautiful girl weeping— please don't ask more, for I cannot tell you what you require of me. It is forbidden." He remained lowered to the ground so as not to frighten her further. "All you need to know is that I am a friend, and I would like to help."

Cecelia shook her head, unexpectedly terrified of the world. Her emotions were too raw from earlier, and trust was not a feeling she was willing to entertain at the moment. She certainly did not want to become reliant upon something that could prove to be a dangerous liaison in the future. If she'd learned one thing within the past several hours, she should never depend upon her instincts, for they would prove to be most undoubtedly wrong.

Her only hope was to now remove herself from the wolf as quickly and as far away as possible. Praying he stayed put and did not attempt to follow her, Cecelia curtsied and thanked the odd creature. "Your inquiries are most graciously received, but I must be gone now. It is very late and I am afraid if I stayed out much longer I would be missed."

Alexander knew any hope of detaining her had passed. She was too distressed, and a sudden move on his part would only alarm the gel more. So he pretended indifference and laid his head upon his paws again. "Very well, you should leave then. It was nice meeting you."

When she turned to go, he called out one last request, "However, if you do find the need to speak to me or would like a listening ear, I come into these woods every night. Leave a small token—perhaps a rose from your mother's garden—upon that stone you were sitting on, and I will be sure to stay and wait for you."

CECELIA NEVER EXPECTED to see the wolf again. Her own world was centered on pleasing her mother and attempting to make the most of her crushed existence after Lord Willington. The last thing she needed was to create clandestine meetings with a beast in which she poured her remorseful little heart out and wept even more.

Instead, she focused her time arranging formal handwritten apologies to all of the guests invited to the nonexistent engagement ball and holding her head up high when those who wished to gossip about her, came as morning callers. Their purpose was to glean information to spread around the village, under the guise of consoling and pitying. It was indeed a sad reality for dear Cecelia, but there was no hope for it. Nothing would bring him back and what's done must be done. She had to make do as best she could and suffer through it as many a young lady had before her, and many a young lady were destined to after her as well. For she was sure handsome young men would never cease to break hearts.

However, it was after a few trying weeks, and a couple of days in particular, where her mother proved to be too much of a nuisance, inviting William's friends over as particular dinner guests to court her forlorn daughter—Cecelia had had enough.

She needed help, advice, something. Someone who could be on her side, someone who would listen to her and not judge or gossip or snicker…she needed a friend.

And it wasn't until that moment, after Lord
Willington left, and after the world divided
itself from her, did she realize she truly did
not have any friend to confide in. No one who
was there just for her. She was lonely and
uncomfortable with the feeling.

Growing up she'd always been well liked
and well talked about, now it would seem
she was only well talked about. Without
her father around as a buffer to life and to
make her laugh and poke fun of herself as he
used to, there were only her own thoughts to
contemplate and peruse.

Many times a day she would be drawn
back to the peculiar short conversation with
the wolf in the forest. Her memory would
naturally settle on them both chuckling at one
another and his soft wit and wry sarcasm.
There was something strangely magnetic about
the beast that drew her thoughts toward him
far more than she was comfortable with. And
yet, once she was away and had examined the
incident with him more fully, she did believe
truly—not just with jaded instincts—but truly
believed, she could trust him. Which is perhaps
what worried her most and kept her away from

him, until now.

With shaking hands she placed her mother's delicate pink rose upon the small boulder she had been sitting on the night she'd met the wolf. The sparkling sunlight broke through the leaves of the trees surrounding the brook and caressed the flower, causing it to glow upon the dark stone. It was simply beautiful, and looked to be a magical good omen of things to come.

Cecelia hastily hurried back toward the house. Her mother had invited another of her brother's friends to dinner and she would have to change soon. She would have naturally dreaded the evening, but the promise of tonight, with the hope of a new friend, altered everything.

She wondered if he would really come.

## Chapter Five

ALEXANDER WANDERED PAST the rose without really noticing it at first. It was a couple of hours before nightfall, and he found himself pent up in the castle and needing to roam while he was still in his human form. Since he first saw Miss Hammerstein-Smythe sitting near the small stream, he had come here often. He made sure it was always during a time when the family would be sitting down to eat, so as not to disrupt her, but he enjoyed feeling the commonality of spirit with such a peaceful place.

The prince had often wondered how she was doing and if she still found the need to

cry all alone. He'd nearly given up hope she
would ever call for him so did not notice the
flower at first. When his brain processed
what it was he saw and recognized there was
something out of place, he turned around and
stared at the rose.

Alexander did not move for a full minute
as he absorbed the fact the delicate pink petals
and thorny stem were indeed in front of him.
And then it hit.

She needed him! She had left the sign
he'd asked her to.

With as much haste as possible, the prince
sped back to the castle and put the rose in a
vase with water. He was eager to do a lot for
her, but what? He needed to think. He needed
to plan and prepare. She required him. She
required a friend. This was his chance to
actually become a true companion as a wolf.
If he could communicate and get someone
to trust him as a beast, then it gave more
optimism for the future than he dared hope for.

The fact this was a girl, who trusted him,
was not lost on the prince either. However,
he had seen his face in the looking glass as an
animal enough to diminish any thoughts of her

falling in love. He'd long given up that hope.
There simply was not a woman in the world
who could love such a hideous monster.

But it didn't stop him from determining
to help her in any way he could. To guarantee
she see him as someone to depend upon.
Someone who was good and kind and all
things normal on this earth, if he could not
give her his soul, then please allow her to
see his true heart. Allow her to see he can be
decent, there was some hope left, and that the
witch was not wholly right.

If he could prove this to someone who
desired his aid, perhaps there would be more
he could do for others later. Much, much later.

WHILE PRINCE ALEXANDER was
preparing for their upcoming meeting in
anxious excitement and wonder, Miss Cecelia
Hammerstein-Smythe was anything but
excited. William's friend, Mr. Velmayne,
was as obnoxious and as proud of himself as
all of her brother's friends proved to be. He
was more interested in sporting events and
racing than the cares of those around him. She

absolutely refused to be associated with idiotic buffoons. And he, in his brightly colored green and yellow waistcoat, pantaloons and jacket, with his ultra-high starched collars looked more of a buffoon than most.

By the time Cecelia saw Mr. Velmayne to the door, she was exceedingly eager to escape to her little brook. Any reservations she had about meeting the beast were long gone with the arrival of her brother's friend. There was nothing she desired more than to vent out her frustrations to someone, anyone with a listening ear at this point.

She was desperate for a friend.

Once the family settled down for the night, and the house quieted, she slipped a gown back over her head, and fastened her boots. Fetching a woolen cape, she was quick to escape the confines of her home and make her way down to the stream. She wondered if the wolf would truly be there.

He was there, waiting for her, and reading a book in the moonlight, no less.

Cecelia was sure he could hear and smell her coming long before she made it close to him, but she decided to announce her arrival anyway. "Well, hello there! You did come and you're reading."

He smiled as well as a wolf could smile and said, "Well, of course I'm here. And did you not think I could read, then?"

She laughed, happy and pleased he continued to be as calm and surprising as he was before. "I've never given it a thought."

"What?" He pulled back and shook his head. "You've never imagined a wolf reading before? I'm appalled."

Cecelia spread her gown around the small boulder and sat down across the brook from him. "So is there anything else you can do that I should be aware of?"

"Miss, are you saying speaking and reading are not enough for my beastly form? I must now perform in other ways as well?"

"Yes." She giggled, lifting her chin and looking down her nose at him. "Yes. I demand that you sing and dance as well."

He grimaced teasingly and glanced back down at his book. "Let me assure you, my howling was not meant for ears as delicate and refined as yours."

Cecelia leaned forward and put her elbows

on her knees. "And your dancing?"

Alexander looked up, his eyes mischievously twinkling in the bluey-darkness. "Now my dancing is something else altogether."

"Really?" Intrigued she wondered what a wolf looked like when he danced.

"Yes, really. Are you perhaps familiar with the expression, 'two left feet'? Well, I have four—paws that is." He waved one for emphasis while Cecelia laughed again.

She loved the charming maturity about him, so very different from William's friends. They would've never admitted to any fault, and yet the wolf did not seem to mind at all. He simply set his paw down and continued to read.

Studying him for a moment she asked, "How do you turn the pages?"

"Very carefully," came the mumbled reply, with his head still down.

"No, I mean honestly, how do you do it?"

He glanced up meeting her eyes briefly. "If you wait, in just a bit, I'll show you."

Cecelia waited. True to his word, less than a minute later, she watched as he used two paws, one to hold the book down on the grass and the other to bow the page and flip it over the other. It was utter brilliance.

"What are you reading?" she had to ask him, curiosity was killing her.

"Something for you. I'm trying to find a passage."

"For me?"

"Yes."

"But why?" She stood up and crossed over the little stream to where the wolf was and sat down next to him, peering over his shoulder.

"Because I thought you needed it, that's why."

"Ugh." She nudged his side with her arm, relishing the soft fur that met her touch. "Are you always this obtuse?"

"Only when being harassed by impatient females." When she smirked out loud, he added, "While I'm looking, will you do something for me?"

"I suppose so, as long as it doesn't involve me chanting to the fairies." Her hand trailed softly over his thick mane.

Cecelia felt the deep rumble in answer and

knew he was trying to hide a chuckle. "Well, that spoils the plan then. Now what should I have you do instead?"

"I know. I could read what's got you so captivated."

"No, I have a better plan. How about you get comfortable while I search and you tell me what's wrong and why you sent for me."

She sighed and tucked her legs up further under her gown. "Does there have to be a reason? Couldn't I just want your adoring company?"

The wolf looked up and over at her, she swore she saw his eyebrow rise. "Tell me what ails you, and then I'll share what I'm searching for."

"That's blackmail!" She laughed, pretending to be scandalized.

"No, my dear, I prefer to call it an even trade. You tell me why you've forced me to sit here at all hours of the night. What would make a beautiful girl so desperate that she would call upon a scary beast for aid? And once this is revealed, I will then show you what I've brought to brighten your mood completely."

Her heart dropped and her hand paused, hovering over his fur. Cecelia's voice was much quieter when she asked, "Have I disturbed you? Do you not wish to be here, then? You don't have to be. It is fine. I'm sure there are many other things you wish you could be doing right now."

"Miss Hammerstein-Smythe, let's get one thing straight." Alexander looked right into her worried eyes. "There is no place I would rather be than right here with you at this moment."

"Really?" She searched his features.

"Yes. Now stop stalling and tell me what's wrong."

# Chapter Six

CECELIA LEANED AGAINST the wolf's soft fuzzy shoulder. He felt so warm and wonderful. "Do you mind if I lay my head upon you?" she asked.

Alexander's heart skipped a beat; she was beginning to trust him. He had to clear his throat before he answered in an even tone, "If it makes you feel more at ease, then by all means indulge yourself."

She turned fully on her back against his thick coat and took in the great forest canopy above her, the stars and moonlight filtering in on little enchanting streams all around them. It was breathtaking and so tranquil. She needed this. She needed serenity more than anything right now.

After a little while of silent contemplation, she asked, "What is your name?"

"You're stalling again," came the mumbled reply.

"Do you have a name?"

He looked up from his reading, not really wanting to answer the question. "Miss Hammerstein-Smythe—"

"Cecelia. My name is Cecelia."

His deep voice vibrated through her as he repeated the name. "Cecelia." He liked the way it rolled off his tongue. It suited her.

"What's yours?"

"I, uh—I don't have one." Alexander was quick to add, "That translates in a language you would understand, of course."

"Oh." She turned her head towards his. "Can I think of one for you?"

"After you tell me what's wrong."

She snorted a very unladylike snort and laughed. "Fine. You win. Where should I start?"

"At the beginning is usually best."

Cecelia took a deep breath. "The

beginning." Her hands clinched the sides of her cloak. "Well, it's not the finest story, I am sure."

"It doesn't have to be. All it has to be is your story. Now, tell me what happened, please."

She took another deep breath and willed herself not to cry as she began, "It's silly really. I must be the most silliest girl in all the kingdom."

"And why is that?" the wolf prodded.

"Because I believed Lord Willington loved me and wanted to marry me."

The imbecile broke her heart? Alexander froze, his ear twitched in agitation, but she did not notice.

"But he did not. He never planned to marry me. All those days, all those dances, all those letters we sent one another were for naught. While I was living in oblivious harmony, he—he was courting, truly courting, his intended—a lady five or ten times my consequence. They are to wed before the summer is over." She paused and blinked back a few stubborn tears. "I feel so foolish. I do not know how it was I could have been so deceived. How could I ever believe he would look twice at me? Of course he would search higher for a bride! Of course he would find one to love who was so much more worthy of him than I."

The beast dared not move, he dared not say a word. After a few moments of silence he was rewarded again with her frustrations.

"Do you know the most humiliating part? I thought—" her voice wobbled, "—I thought he was taking me out to propose. We all did. The whole village believed I would become the intended of Lord Willington when he took me driving in his open carriage. Except it was to announce his intentions to wed another, not me. I had no idea until that moment when he crushed all of my hopes and dreams in a matter of seconds. I did not let him see me as a watering pot, I held in my tears until much later that night. The night you found me all alone here. My world had ended that day. Everything and everyone I'd ever trusted dissolved in front of my eyes.

"I loved him enough to want him happy. I needed him happy, but at what cost? I would give anything to rewind the past and not allow my heart the freedom it so willingly took in attaching itself to Charles."

Alexander's chest was cold. He felt for the girl, but did wonder at her stupidity in choosing such a fop as Lord Willington. The man was more ego than brains—

The wolf's thoughts ended abruptly when he realized he used to be just like the man who shattered Miss Hammerstein-Smythe. And five months ago, had he been so inclined, Alexander would have had no qualms in doing something in a similar fashion to her as well. In fact, hadn't he been more cruel than most? He winced at the memory of their last meeting. She in the town hall aiding the pianist, who was to perform later that evening, with some salve for her arthritic hands, and he on an errand to deliver papers to the mayor and hoping to catch a quick word with him. Alexander had stumbled upon her quite easily enough; he was told the man had last been seen in the concert room. So when he interrupted Miss Hammerstein-Smythe rubbing the old woman's hands gently he began to snigger—loudly.

Cecelia's head had snapped up and she

glared at him over the pianoforte. She was the only person who was not afraid to put him in his place. "Will you kindly reserve your usual lack of decorum for those who appreciate it?"

He had laughed and shook his head, tapping the papers in his hand against his side. "Do you honestly believe you will ever find a life worth living if all you do is go about meddling with everyone else's?" He walked forward and rested his elbow upon the pianoforte while sneering down at her. "You disgust me, and I rue the day any man would be foolish enough to align himself with you."

Her jaw tightened, which proved his words had fully hit their mark. He went in for the kill before she could react properly and lambast him, "Pardon me! What am I thinking? Why would anyone care for such a female as you? They would have to be imbeciles themselves to consider the notion. Think of the pain you would put them through! The agonies! The heartache! Oh, to look at such a face as yours across the breakfast table every morning would be horrendous indeed."

"To look at my face?" Her voice lowered. "You are the monster here. Mayhap you

are handsome, but with your personality no
woman in her proper mind would consider
herself stupid enough to be in the same room
with you, let alone the same house!"

As she quickly scurried and gathered up
her things, he knew he had finally gotten under
her skin. When she gave the woman a hug,
whispering a quick farewell and then turning
toward the prince, bowing low, he enjoyed
her hasty retreat out the door and he grinned,
knowing then he had just secured another good
month at least before she would fall for him.

Except, she was smarter—much smarter—
she never did fall for Prince Alexander's
prideful notions and preening. Instead she
allowed herself to be swallowed up by a
different prey altogether.

"Miss—Cecelia?" the wolf whispered.

She sniffed and then answered against his
side, "Yes?"

He opened his mouth to speak, his paw
marking the page in the book, but no words
would come out. There was so much he
longed to say, yet none of it seemed suitable.
Instead he asked, "What happened then? What
did the village people do? Were they kind?"

She turned and curled into a tight ball, facing him, still resting upon his side. He knew she was lying simply by her actions.

"They—they were supportive and good and everything gracious."

"Indeed?"

"Yes, I have never known such an outpouring of compassion."

"Cecelia?"

"Hmm?"

"Tell me the truth. What actually happened?"

She buried her face into his soft coat and mumbled, "Go away."

"No. Tell me. Get it out, my dear."

She chuckled into his side. "Has anyone ever complained of how aggravating you can be?"

"Many times."

She grumbled and groaned and then finally said, "It was dreadful." Pulling her cloak around her she continued, "They have only come to glean information and secretly mock me when my back is turned. I have become the village idiot, their laughingstock. All those I considered my friends are more eager to watch and croon over my failure than to sympathize with me." Her voice quieted. "They saw what I did not, and they were right. I am as worthless to them as I am to Lord Willington. Without his approval I shall never have theirs."

Alexander could not pinpoint what changed his opinion of this brave girl so fully, other than her trust in him, but he found himself vowing to right every wrong in her life. He found his heart beating in response to her pain, his need to maintain and strengthen her. And he felt much of this guilt was resting upon his shoulders—his constant treatment of her publicly weighed heavily in this too. How else would a village react to a girl when their own prince does not care for her?

A month ago she was as happy and confident and carefree as anyone he knew— nosy and prodding and continually on her quest to help everyone around her. Now when she needed them most, her friends—in their pride and jealousy—had turned their backs on her and left Miss Hammerstein-Smythe to see the cruel world for what it was.

He had so much to make up for; he

deserved this face, this body, this curse—when he thought back on what he had carelessly done to her. He had to reverse this wrong. This was not the way things were done.

And Prince Alexander Henry Richard the Fourth would see that every available comfort was given her. He would have her stand again within the walls of her village. No one should be mocking someone so kindhearted and naturally good-natured. He understood now her easy smile and quick laughter proved her disposition to be one of great worth. Many people would grow stronger and happier within themselves had they half her optimism and gumption. How would his own outcome have been had he heeded her perfect example?

The world was not right if Cecelia Hammerstein-Smythe was hurt. Nothing seemed to make sense. Her generous nosy habits needed to be applauded and adored, not hidden away.

But what could he do? What could a mere wolf do to improve the situation?

He cleared his throat, hoping she had not been concerned over his silence. She did not seem to be so, appearing deep in thought herself. "Well, to thank you for your admission, would you like to read what I have found?"

Cecelia brightened immediately and quickly sat up. "Yes, please."

"Very well." He passed the book over, careful to not lose the spot. "You see the paragraph starting just there?" he asked as he pointed with his paw.

"Yes."

"Good. Read the next little bit. You will know when to stop."

"Do you mean for me to read aloud?"

"If you desire."

She snuggled her feet under her gown. Finding a glimmer of moonlight, she held the book up and began to read out loud—

*Oh, hark! Thy little wingless bird,*
*For beauty takes its flight—*
*If thou were but ten feet tall,*
*Thy strength would own the night.*
*But alas, thy fragile wings are small.*
*And so must thy courage ground*
*My modest passing bonny brow*
*If thou could but see thy crown!*

*The land would forge ever onward*
*Pressing gloriously within sight*
*For thee, my precious moonbeam*
*Will yet prevail the fight.*

After a moment of contemplation, she spoke. "You are telling me to not give up hope, aren't you?"

"I am telling you, you are worth more than you believe you are."

She blushed and shook her head, grateful for the darkness. "Why is it when the wolf says it I almost believe him?"

He grinned a wolfish grin. "Girls in forests should always believe what magical beasts say."

She rubbed her lips together, worry lines appeared between her eyes. "Why?"

"Because I care." Alexander sat up on his back haunches. "Because when you do not believe it exists, I see the crown upon your brow."

"I don't understand; how could I be worth more than what people see me as?" She drew her legs up and rested her head upon them. "Isn't something only worth what someone is willing to spend for it?"

"I would spend the prince's fortune for you, if I had to."

Cecelia laughed. "And what would the lofty Prince Alexander say to such a ploy?" She smoothed her skirts and wrapped her arms around her legs. "Perhaps you didn't know, but he does not think my worth is that great either. You see? I am hopeless cause." A ragged sigh escaped. "In fact, there is not one person who feels as you do." Her voice broke. "Then again, they know me and you do not."

His heart lodged within his throat at the sight of her valiantly blinking away tears. "You are wrong, my dear, and I will prove it to you. I know you greater than I know myself."

Her watery eyes met his deep steady gaze.

She drew strength from that gaze; he did not flinch or waver.

"Mark my words, little wingless bird, you will fly."

She inhaled a shaky breath. "Thank you. I do not know what delicious sprite of fate brought you here, but thank you. I have never needed anything more."

Alexander nodded his head. He knew. He

knew exactly what she was going through—
didn't he just go through his own painful
growing trial? And yet, his was deserved, hers
was not.

"Cecelia, I promise, starting tomorrow
everything will change for you."

# Chapter Seven

AT ELEVEN O'CLOCK the next morning, Cecelia's house was in deep uproar. The maids, the footmen, Sanford, Mrs. Parnel—the cook, Mrs. Hammerstein-Smythe and William were all in great agitation. For about two full minutes no one knew quite what to do. It wasn't until the lady of the house took control and demanded that one of the maids go and wake her daughter immediately and see that she was dressed properly, that the house began to move again. She had barked several more orders out before all was completely to her satisfaction—

"Sanford, see that he is brought into the

best parlor and make sure there is at least one footman to attend him, send in Harold, he will do the best and looks the sharpest in his uniform."

"Cook, get the finest tea set down and get those extra footmen to help you clean them. Prepare something for a feast—but make it elegant! And make sure he has some sort of nourishment now, for who knows how long it will take Cecelia to get ready, let alone wake up. I cannot gather she has slept at all last evening."

"Matilda and Penelope, I want you both upstairs with me and Cecelia. We must have our hair done splendidly."

"William! You get dressed into something decent, not that old coat, and go and entertain him until we can join you. Now. Oh! And make sure Dawkins has shined your nice boots as well."

By the time Mrs. Hammerstein-Smythe had made it up the stairs, the special guest's horse had been stabled and he'd been ushered into the best parlor with the footman and a small tray of finger foods cook had miraculously thrown together and artfully

arranged. Tea was brewing, and the feast was
in its beginning preparations while Cecelia
was just then stretching awake from her long
night out with the beast.

"I'm sorry, who did you say was here?"

"The Prince, Miss." Matilda bobbed a
curtsy. "He came all the way from his castle
this very morning to see you."

Cecelia sat straight up in her bed, wide
awake now. "Is this some jest of William's?"

"No, Miss. He's in the best parlor now
with your brother attending him. But he came
with the express desire to see you."

"Me? Me?! Are you sure?"

"Positive, Miss. Mrs. Hammerstein-
Smythe is completely out of sorts over it
and has declared you must be dressed and
downstairs as soon as possible."

"Oh, great heavens!" Cecelia grumbled
as she stepped out of her warm bed and began
changing with the help of Matilda and Sally,
her usual maid. "I wonder what in the world
the man wants? He's never once singled me
out before."

Her mother burst into the room in a sea of
elegant red satin and gold fobs, as Cecelia was

in front of the looking glass getting her hair done.

"Oh, good, I see that you've already started dressing. The blue one is an excellent choice as well, shows off your features and handsome figure perfectly." Her mother crossed to her jewelry box and began digging inside. "Here is a pretty set of pearls, not too much for this early in the morning, I don't think—at least when one is entertaining a prince." She clasped them around Cecelia's neck while Matilda moved to the side, still holding a lock of unruly hair she'd been taming down.

"Mother, I don't think we need to go to this much trouble. I'm sure he's not here for very long anyway."

"Cecelia, you will do as you're told and look your best. You must make the most of this fortunate opportunity. Oh, how I cannot wait to see the looks on the Smithfields' faces when they learn who our important visitor was this morning." She smiled down at her daughter through the reflection. "And to think you, of all the girls here, was the one to capture Prince Alexander's fancy."

"Mother! I did not capture his fancy. He does not even care for me. I have no idea why he's come today, but I assure you, it is not at all what you think. And I would appreciate it greatly if you did not spread this about the neighborhood. I've already had to deal with one rejection and the aftermath of gossip, I certainly do not want to deal with the whole village babbling on about how the prince does not pay me any more attention after today."

Cecelia's words were short lived as she made her way into the best parlor and was met by an overly charming prince.

"Miss Hammerstein-Smythe, so good to see you!" Alexander stood and bowed as she came into the room and then he nodded toward her mother. He surprisingly walked right up to Cecelia and held her hand and directed her to the large opulent blue velvet chair opposite his.

Her mother nearly tripped she was so stunned by his exacting attention to her daughter, especially after the monologue Cecelia had blurted out earlier. Here was a man most decidedly interested in her child, no matter what she said about it.

Mrs. Hammerstein-Smythe opted to perch herself on the matching sofa and directed her son, who had stood when the women walked in the room, to do the same.

The prince had no eyes or cares, beyond common courtesy, for anyone but Cecelia and proved this by nearly singling her out completely with conversation only she could answer from the moment she sat down.

"Blue suits you very well; do you wear the gown often?"

She blinked and looked down at her dress. "Thank you. I don't particularly wear this one much."

"And did you sleep well last night, Miss Hammerstein-Smythe?"

"I, uh—yes, I did. Very well, thank you."

"And do you find the weather recently to your liking?"

"The weather?" Cecelia was at a loss as to why he was speaking about such things. "Yes, the weather has been very fine." What was going on here? She looked back up and met a distinct sparkle in his eye. *Was he teasing me?* Cecelia was keen to ask him some personal questions of her own. Like, why was he here?

What did he want? And just what cruel jest would he make of her this time?

Glancing at her mother and brother, she noticed they were both staring straight at them. Of course they were! What else was there to look at? She was trapped. She very well could not ask him what she wanted to with her family looking on. Her mother would more than likely have an apoplectic fit if she knew even half of what Cecelia was thinking right now.

"Prince Alexander, since you've been speaking of the weather, it's made me long for the outdoors. Would you perhaps mind escorting me while we stroll among my mother's rose garden?"

Mrs. Hammerstein-Smythe gasped in shock. She was stunned her daughter could be so presumptuous and forward to invite the prince for a stroll.

Cecelia did feel a momentary stab of guilt for being so brazen, but she could not think of another way to get him alone at the moment.

However, Prince Alexander was more than pleased to oblige, so there was no lasting damage done in her mother's eyes. "I would be delighted to do just that very thing. In fact, I had been contemplating how to ask you, so I am grateful you thought to do so yourself."

Cecelia did not believe a word he spoke, but was satisfied he was willing to play along so well. With a small smile to her mother and a nod to William, she stood after such a short time, and was escorted out on the arm of the prince to the entranceway of the great house. There she was met by her maid, with a matching blue bonnet and pelisse. She quickly slipped both on, and allowed herself to hang upon the prince's arm a moment more until they were out in the garden at last, before pulling away from him.

"Do you feel better?" he asked before she'd begun her questioning.

"No, I do not feel better." She ducked behind a high rosebush, away from the window's view and planted her hands upon her hips and hissed, "What are you doing here?"

Alexander joined her, and smiled. "Irritating you, of course."

"Well!" Cecelia's jaw dropped briefly, before she gathered her wits about her. "You're doing a very fine job of it." When he laughed in response, she asked, "No, honestly, why are you here? It is no secret how we feel about each other, and you know what this will do to the village. Already tongues will begin wagging before you've been here an hour. They will all wonder why you have come to see me and what your intentions are." She folded her arms and agitatingly tapped one small foot upon the cobblestone path.

The irksome man grinned a very dashing grin while raising an eyebrow and said, "What if I want them to wonder? What if I'm hoping they see me here and they talk about us?"

Her heart dropped, she felt almost ill. "Please, my prince, please." She took a step forward and laid one hand upon his arm. "I entreat you, I beg of you, don't. I could not bear to be the laughingstock of this town." Not again. She glanced down, frantic not to meet his gaze. She had simply no pride left. "If you must have your sport, can it not be with another girl? I know you feel nothing for me. I know you detest me as much as I detest you. Please, I beg of you, do not do this."

"Miss Hammerstein-Smythe," the prince tucked a finger under her chin and gently brought her face to meet his dark brown gaze. "I am different now. I would never do anything to harm you. I assure you with all my heart, it is the least of my intentions."

Bewildered, she asked, "Why are you here, then?"

# Chapter Eight

THE PRINCE LOOKED down at her delightful features and reluctantly removed his finger from her chin. He placed his hands behind his back and took a couple of steps forward and away from the girl, pleased to see her following. "It would seem you and I have a mutual friend."

"We do?" asked Cecelia, not certain how this could pertain to his delight in tormenting her.

Alexander peeked around a few of the bushes surrounding them, making certain no one was listening, and then stepped toward her, his deep baritone whispering in her ear. "A magical friend."

Cecelia gasped, not sure if it was from the close proximity of the prince, or from what he had said. Either way, it took a few moments to catch her breath. When she was finally able she hesitantly whispered back, "Do you mean an animal friend?"

Prince Alexander swayed under the onslaught of her sweet warm breath just below his ear. Before he realized what he was meaning to do he'd grabbed her shoulders for support. Clearing his throat he answered, "Yes. A wolf who can speak." Good great grief, he was dizzy. The girl merely asked him a question and near enough brought him to his knees. What had come over him? He'd never before felt such an attraction, and he wondered briefly if he was falling in love with her.

"Prince Alexander?"

Cecelia's voice brought him back to the present. He looked down at her rose-colored lips and watched as her teeth tugged and pulled at the bottom one. "Yes?" he asked a bit mesmerized.

"You're holding my shoulders very tightly."

"I am?"

"Mm-hm…are you all right?"

Her blue eyes were endless. Had he never noticed the color of her eyes before? "Better than I've ever been." He leaned down and kissed the girl right on her perfect lips. They were as soft and as sweet as he imagined.

Cecelia quickly pulled out of his arms. "Prince Alexander! What in the world has come over you?"

He wanted to taste her lips again. "I don't know. I don't think I'm fully sound at the moment."

She was surprised when a giggle popped out of her. Never had she seen him look so bewildered. "You simply cannot go about kissing girls in their mother's rose garden during broad daylight. It is just not done. Especially ones you feel nothing for and could care less about." Her hand unconsciously touched her tingling lips, marveling at the sensation he was able to create.

Appalled at how ungentlemanly she must think him now, he immediately began to apologize. "My dear Miss Hammerstein-Smythe, you must forgive me—"

Her blue eyes turned to steel. "If you say one more word I'll box your ears."

Alexander's eyebrows rose.

"No, sir. You do not get to now tell me how deeply sorry you are for ruining my life. Indeed you did not ruin my life, you simply enhanced it."

"Enhanced it?" He pursed his mouth together to prevent the grin from forming.

"Yes." She bit her lip again to stop her own chuckle. "It was very nice, and I am not sorry it happened. However, you can never do it again."

"Never?" He took a step forward.

She laughed and put a hand between them. "Never, ever again."

"And why is that?" asked the prince coyly.

"Because you and I despise each other and always have. Besides, then everyone would assume we were engaged."

Engaged.

To Miss Cecelia Hammerstein-Smythe.

Princess Cecelia.

His princess.

He had never wanted anything more.

While Alexander's heart was learning how

to beat properly again, Cecelia had obliviously and quite cheerfully continued to chatter as she began to search for the perfect rose.

"So how did you meet the wolf? Isn't he simply astonishing? Did you know he can read? It was so inconceivable to see him lying down and reading a book when I met with him last night. I've never encountered a magical creature like him before, have you?"

She stopped and turned, a beautiful yellow rose in her hand. "Prince Alexander?"

He shook his head and stepped forward. "Uh, yes?"

"Have you?"

He sheepishly grinned, looking like a boy in a top hat and princely finery. "I'm sorry, I wasn't attending. What did you ask of me?"

Puzzled, she glanced over him. "Did you hear none of it, then?"

Alexander put his hands behind his back and admitted, "None."

"Oh." Cecelia looked at him peculiarly for a moment and then said, "I guess what I wanted to know most was, how do you know the wolf?"

He'd been pondering that exact same

question, knowing without a doubt she would ask it of him, so he was definitely prepared to answer it. "I came across him one evening in the woods a while ago. We've been friends ever since."

"Isn't he fascinating?"

Alexander shrugged and then nodded. "Yes, I guess that's a good word for him."

"Were you startled when he began talking to you?"

The prince chuckled. "Yes. I was grateful he spoke, actually. Because it proved he could communicate and wouldn't eat me."

Cecelia laughed and continued on down the path, the prince close beside her.

"Did he frighten you?" He watched her closely.

"Yes. He did a little." She slowed and turned more fully toward him, her skirts swirling below her. "But then, I don't know what happened, when I looked back and replayed the meeting over and over again, I just knew I could trust him."

"Good. You can always trust him." He touched the soft petal of a yellow rose next to him as he walked past. "Do not doubt he is the most dependable creature you will ever come across."

It was interesting to see Prince Alexander so serious and calm. Honestly, she could hardly believe he was the same person she'd met previously. There really was something most decidedly different about the man. "I like that you know him, and can vouch for him," she said as she followed his example and trailed her fingers lightly over the rosebushes as they walked.

"You do?"

"Yes. I do not understand why, but it makes me appreciate you more that we share the same friend."

"Does he mean that much to you, then?" Alexander stopped breathing as he awaited her reply.

Cecelia paused, her fingers absentmindedly caressing a small leaf. "I don't know." She continued to step forward again, allowing the leaf to be plucked. "He has the potential to be someone I care about, yes. So maybe that's it?"

Could she really be saying what he thought she was? Could this sweet girl before him truly not judge a hideous wolf and see him as an equal, as a friend? As someone she could care for? The prince watched in wonder and silence for a few minutes as he absorbed all the magnificence that was Miss Hammerstein-Smythe. She was an even greater person than he could have imagined.

Cecelia's thoughts naturally gravitated toward the enigmatic wolf. Never had she met someone so fascinating before, or so kind. A smile played upon her lips as she thought of the passage of poem he had had her read aloud. How had he known the precise thing to say to her when she needed it most? How could anyone, let alone a beast, know her so well?

She walked forward a few more steps and plucked another leaf before her feet stopped altogether. What did he mean when he said today would change everything in my life? Glancing at the profile of the prince she absentmindedly mulled over the cryptic comment from the wolf before she silently gasped. The beast sent the prince. He would not dare do such a thing! She began to walk again. And yet, it would seem he had done just that. Her hands grew cold as she realized that the dear creature she had begun to trust had indeed betrayed her.

"He told you about me, did he not?" she asked rather quietly.

Alexander glanced over. "The wolf?"

"Yes." She took a deep breath and stopped walking altogether. The more she thought about it, the more bothered she became. Everything they had just been discussing, all the camaraderie she'd felt with the prince, vanished before her eyes. "He told you about me—about what had happened to me—which is why you have come here now, to rescue the poor damsel and make sure all the village believes you are courting her, and in love with her. The beast said before I left last night that today would change everything in my life. He meant you, didn't he? He meant to come to you and tell you all about my wretched existence, so that way you would take pity and help."

"Would it be so bad if he did?"

"Yes!" Distressed, she looked away.

He stepped in front of her. "Why?"

"Because—because, it's you! Because

you have never taken a moment out of your life to say one good thing about anyone, least of all me. Because I am humiliated beyond belief you know about my trials and heartaches. Someone who has only ever scorned and mocked me publically now comes in as my great prince on a white horse."

"Miss Hammerstein-Smythe, please, you said so yourself just a few weeks ago that I have changed. I did not own it then, but believe me, my dear, I have. I know I have." He shockingly knelt down in front of her, placed the rose she was holding on the ground near her feet, and took her hands. "Allow me this opportunity now, for if you will not accept my friendship, then please accept my apologies. My dearest, most sincere apologies for everything—all those cruel days of my past—I was a monster. I was a horrendous, horrid beastly monster, and I treated you abominably. I will forever be in your debt, Miss Hammerstein-Smythe, if you could but forgive me and see that I am and will always be a changed man."

She squeezed his hands not quite willing to let the fight go. "You were brutal to me."

"Yes, I was. And to many more people, as well. I would do anything to go back and change it all now—anything."

She searched and wandered across his earnest attractive features. "How can I trust you?"

"Have we not had a pleasant time these past twenty minutes or so? Can this not prove that we can get along? That maybe I am not as ghastly as I once was?"

A lopsided grin formed upon her lips. "Perhaps not as ghastly."

In all tender seriousness he said, "I am sorry. I am wholeheartedly, earnestly, profusely sorry. And I vow, if you allow me, to make it up to you every single day of my life."

"Did the beast really send you?"

"Yes, he did."

She sighed in frustration before stating, "You are forgiven. I will proceed to allow you to rescue me, and perhaps become your friend. However—" she raised an eyebrow to ward off his happy smile—"I'm pretty positive tonight I shall taste my first wolf stew."

Alexander threw his head back and

laughed, more in love with her than before.

It was at this exact moment, while the prince was kneeling before Cecelia— with a rose lying between them and their hands clasped tightly—looking like the happiest man on earth, that her mother happened upon them both.

"Cecelia! Cecelia, my dearest girl! You are to be married to the prince?! My daughter, the soon-to-be queen!" she exclaimed loudly, in all the ecstasies of a mother's wildest dreams coming true, before she swooned and crashed gracefully upon the cobblestones before them.

# Chapter Nine

PRINCE ALEXANDER WAS still chuckling over Cecelia's shocked countenance at her mother's announcement and then dramatic fall as he rode his horse, Sterling, home. You would have thought someone had slapped Miss Hammerstein-Smythe, she was so appalled.

He was not appalled. He should have been. But he wasn't.

In fact, the sweet irony of the situation did much to please him in his good humor as he travelled back to the castle. He would've loved to have stayed longer, just to guarantee those rumors spread like wildfire even faster than they were already going, but he had a meeting with his cousin, the Grand Duke, Lord Bellemount—heir to his throne—within the hour and so could not waste another minute.

He did, however, allow his thoughts to roam with great care over the delightfulness of Cecelia. How could he not? Never had he met a female more enchanting than her, and he'd be a simpleton not to spend a good portion of his day thinking about her.

It was very, very true. He wanted to marry the gel.

He needed to marry her, so he could wake up each morning and see what it was she would do or say that would make him laugh. Oh, how she made him laugh! How she made his heart prick into consciousness whenever she was around. He wanted to be a better man for her. He needed to be. He wanted to slay all her dragons and show her the carefree beauty of the world.

He needed Cecelia like he'd never needed any girl before.

She was lively, and endearing, and strong, and humorous, and simply charming.

Alexander was so busy allowing his mind

to wander over the past memories of her that he did not fully acknowledge the pickle he'd placed himself in for quite some time. Indeed, it was not until his horse was entering into the castle courtyard that the smallest fissure of doubt crept into his thoughts at all. But when it came crashing into his euphoria, it did take hold and lay claim to all other previous moments of happiness and perfection.

For in that instant he realized he would never own her. She would never become his because she would have to be in love with the beast for him to break the spell. And yet, he had just entangled them both in a very large and scandalous "imaginary engagement," that the whole village was speaking of. He was in love with her as the prince and the wolf, but she—she may become forced out of propriety's sake to accept a real proposal of marriage from the prince. If he did not propose now, how much worse would the ramifications be? If Prince Alexander walked away, hoping to court her as an impossible beast, wouldn't her life be over? Would not the town destroy what little bit of dignity and gaiety and laughter she had left? It would ruin her for sure.

And yet, if he did not, how could he live without her forever? In just over six months, he would evermore remain a hideous beast without any chance of regaining normalcy again.

She, in the end, would lose him anyway.

And he would lose her.

Gah! Prince Alexander dismounted from Sterling and shook his head to chase away the frustrations. He needed to clear his mind for his meeting with Lord Bellemount in a few minutes. Leaving the stables, he quickly changed into clean clothes—deciding something less "princely" and more "normal" would be best for his cousin the duke.

By the time he'd made it back downstairs and into the great room, Lord Bellemount was already waiting for him. "So there you are!" his cousin exclaimed as he came into the room.

"Here I am." Alexander smiled. "Have you been waiting long?"

"Not as long as I would have preferred to." Bellemount smirked and nodded his head to the side. "Your maid is quite fetching."

Alexander watched as the pretty maid blushed and then dipped into a curtsy. "You're welcome to go, Madeline. Tell my mother I'll be in here with Lord Bellemount for a good hour or so."

"Yes, your highness." She curtsied again and scurried out.

Alexander watched his cousin closely. "You didn't do anything to the poor girl, did you?"

Bellemount laughed and shrugged, looking everything but innocent. "And what would I do within the walls of the castle, knowing you would be joining me soon?" He chuckled as if he knew something the prince did not.

"Frederick." Alexander called him by the name his cousin had detested since childhood. "If you even lay a finger on the gel, I'll chop it off."

"I vow I did not touch her. I only flirted a bit and made her blush. She is very sweet."

"She is also very off limits." The prince found a chair and sat down facing his cousin.

Frederick followed suit and sprawled out upon the large sofa. "Admit it, cuz. You've thought about kissing her more than once."

Images of Cecelia's perfect lips sprung to Alexander's mind. He smiled.

"Aha!" crowed Lord Bellemount, "I knew you had. I can tell you have just by your smile."

Alexander simply stated, "Then you would be wrong. I have never looked at Madeline in that light and I never will."

"Then who made you smile just then?" he asked, thinking perhaps to ferret out of the prince that indeed he was thinking of the maid.

"A beautiful girl."

Frederick's chest tightened and he quickly sat up. "What are you talking about? I mean, who are you talking about?" This could not be, he could not be falling in love now. Not now, not when Frederick was so close to actually having the throne abdicated to him. It was no secret Alexander hoped to do just that and soon, though Lord Bellemount pretended not to know anything of the kind. It simply would not do if he showed too much interest. But, curses! That was his throne, and he'd be good and sure no upstart girl, who would hope to raise a family one day and have heirs of her own, got between him and his dream.

Lord Bellemount realized Alexander still hadn't said anything. The prince serenely sat across from him with a look he'd never seen before. A look that guaranteed his worst fears; his cousin was indeed deeply troubled and deeply in love.

"Ahem." Frederick cleared his throat, trying again. "So who is this beautiful girl that has you so silent this afternoon?" He would find her and destroy her the first moment he had.

"Am I silent?"

"Yes." Lord Bellemount chuckled uneasily. "You look like a man who could use some advice. Do you need help with something?"

Alexander closed his eyes briefly. He needed so much help. He needed advice more than any man. How he wished he knew what to do about Cecelia.

"Cuz, what is it? What's wrong?" Frederick could feel the prince shifting. Another few nudges and he knew he'd open up and tell him who it was that was ruining everything. "Is it the girl you think is so beautiful? Has she upset you or something?"

"Huh?" Alexander rubbed his face with one hand and stared at his cousin a moment before saying, "No. She hasn't upset me, just the opposite."

"She has made you happy?" Frederick asked, not sure where his cousin was going with the conversation.

"No. I'm about to make her very upset soon, though, unless I can come up with a solution." Prince Alexander was just about to open up and tell Frederick as much as he could about Cecelia, without revealing his own part as a wolf, when his cousin burst out almost frantically—

"What is her name?"

Alexander blinked at his tone. "Why?"

"Just tell me who the girl is." Frederick crossed his arms and demanded a second time, "What is her name?"

The prince slowly sat up and leaned forward, his voice measured. "Again, I ask you, why?"

"Because I need to know exactly what is going on here, if I'm to help you." Lord Bellemount smiled, but his foot began to tap irritation. He could hardly sit still with all of the thoughts of what he'd like to do to the girl roaming around his head. "What is her name?"

Alexander examined his cousin closely before lying quite bluntly, "I don't know her name."

Frederick looked like he was about to burst. "What do you mean you don't know her name?"

"It means I do not know her name. She's someone I have met recently, and I do not know her name." His voice was calm and measured.

"That's ridiculous! Everyone knows everyone around here." Lord Bellemount stood up. "Where is she from? Do I know the village?"

Alexander stood up with Frederick and opened his hands in a helpless gesture. "I'm afraid I don't know where she's from either."

"Are you jesting?"

"No, I'm not." It was time to put an end to this charade of a meeting. The prince stepped up and put his arm around his cousin's shoulder. "And actually, you'll have to forgive me. I completely forgot about another engagement I had—something I promised to do for someone. Thank you so much for stopping by." He tugged gently and walked forward, forcing Frederick out of the room with him. "I'm sure you can find your own way out."

"But I thought you were anxious to speak to me about a matter of great importance?"

"I was. I am," he answered, barely keeping his temper in check, while steering him toward the main hall. "But it will have to be another day. Forgive me." With that, Alexander was racing up the stairs to his rooms, leaving Frederick to see himself out of the castle. He would be hanged the day he gave his cousin one ounce of information about Miss Hammerstein-Smythe! There was absolutely no reason why his own cousin should become hostile at the mention of a girl in Alexander's life. He wasn't quite sure what was wrong, but he certainly wasn't about to leave the only woman he'd ever loved vulnerable to such a man. The man he'd hoped to announce—this very afternoon—would be taking up his throne in six months time!

Something was not right and he vowed he would get to the bottom of it before any such announcements or family introductions were made.

Prince Alexander wasn't the only one making vows at that moment. Down below, in another part of the great castle, Lord Bellemount was making his own plans.

There was something decidedly false in the way the prince had evaded his questions just now and then conveniently remembered another commitment. Frederick had no idea what was going on, but he was positive Alexander not only knew the girl's name, but where she lived as well. He'd bet his right foot on it!

The only thing to do now was wait and watch. With a smirk and a raise of his eyebrow, Lord Bellemount slipped to another part of the castle altogether—a long secret passage—and exited outside, through an opening of the garden statue. It was the perfect spot to watch all the comings and goings of the palace without being spotted, which was exactly what he needed to do. One way or another he would find out who this girl was and then she would be dead.

Frederick smiled. The poor prince would be in such an anguished state of losing his only love. Once she died, he would have nothing left within him to run the country and so would naturally abdicate to me.

He hunkered down and prepared himself for a long wait. This was most definitely going to be worth it.

# Chapter Ten

CECELIA MARCHED DOWN to the brook as soon as she had a free moment to herself. Her mother would hardly let the matter of the "supposed engagement" go long enough to leave her alone for a time.

She was going to skin that wolf alive!

Clutching the yellow rose, she veered down the path at record speeds. How dare he mention anything of their private conversations with anyone? And how dare he have the presumption to play matchmaker—or more like pity-maker—without her approval first. Of all the ridiculous harebrained schemes to come up with, sending the great

Prince Alexander to rescue her had to be at the top of the idiocy chain!

And now look at the mess she was in.

The moronic prince refused to even refute one felicitous exclamation of joy in their honor! He sat with complete composure and a smile on his face, as if he were not fully aware of what was happening all around them. As if he did not for one moment realize the immense scandal and horrendousness that was about to unfold.

Once her mother had fallen, the serenity of the moment was completely gone. Gardeners, maids, footmen, stable boys, even the cook and Sanford came to see what the fuss was about. It took several people, including the prince, to remove her distraught mother to the chaise lounge in the blue parlor and revive her. But once she was fully herself again, Cecelia only wished her right back to oblivion. No sooner had she awoken did she begin to exclaim over the engagement once more. Except for this time it was in front of several onlookers!

And the inane prince should have his brains examined for the nonchalant way he sat

there and grinned making a fool of Cecelia's
protests. Every time she would explain
they were not engaged and her mother had
misinterpreted, the buffoon would hold her
hand and look deeply into her eyes, causing all
the women in the room to swoon in giddiness.

Good great heavens!

She should strangle them both.

Cecelia placed the rose high upon the
stone, guaranteeing it would not be missed.
There was much she wanted to say to the beast
and was grateful she had a few hours to put
her thoughts together. As quickly as she'd
come to the little stream, she made her way
back. She did not have the luxury of blissful
contemplation. Her mother would never allow
her away from the house that long. The only
way she'd be able to spend any time at the
brook today would be later that night with the
beast.

She'd never wished for anything more.

By the time Cecelia had managed to make
her way down to the stream later that evening,
it was well past ten o'clock and Alexander
had been there over an hour. He hadn't been
sure what to do for her, and had spent a good

deal of time sorting through the things in his possession to come up with something that might ease her anger a bit. He'd settled upon a heart-shaped locket, which was held together by a rose that doubled as a lock. There was a trick to the catch and one would not know the heart even opened, if they didn't identify the secret.

Inside he had written on a small scroll of paper, with fine penmanship, a portion of the very poem he'd found for her the last time she had met him as a wolf, as well as a simple note from himself. The prince was not sure if he would tell her about the hidden compartment, wondering if she would find it herself. He decided it was best to see how she accepted the gift of the necklace first. He tucked the heart under a small patch of clover for the perfect opportunity to reveal it to her.

"So, you did not bring a book today?" she asked as she approached and settled herself upon the rock.

"No. I brought something better." He was again waiting for her on the other side of the brook, lying on his stomach.

"It is something I can hit you with?" she

smiled as she said it, but there was a certain gleam in her eye in the moonlight.

He tilted his head. "Perhaps, though I believe you won't find it as satisfying as a book would have been."

"Pity."

"Are you very angry with me, then?"

Cecelia brought her knees up and wrapped her arms around her legs. "You could describe my emotions as such."

The beast sighed and laid his head upon his paws. "Out with it, we might as well get this over with now."

She opened her mouth to speak, but caught a glimpse of his dark brown eyes looking up from his dejected position. "Oh, goodness, do not look at me like that. How am I supposed to reprimand you when you use those eyes on me?"

"What? What am I doing?" Alexander titled his head and made his expression even more forlorn.

Cecelia laughed and threw a tuft of grass at him across the water. "It will not do. You cannot make me laugh; I must say these things to you."

The wolf chuckled into his paws. "No one is stopping you."

"Argh." She made a very unladylike grunt, promptly got up, and cautiously stepped over the stream, then without further ado curled up against his side and snuggled into his soft fur. "You are the most incorrigible monster that has ever roamed this land."

"I know," he said softly, loving the feel of her warmth beside him.

"Hmm…" Her soft muffled words could barely be heard. "Horrendous beast, I should beat you to a pulp right now."

"Yes, you should."

"Merk." She rolled to her back against his and looked up at the twinkling stars. "Do not agree with me. It takes all the fun out of arguing."

"Should I not?"

"No, you shouldn't."

He smiled. "What ought I to do then? Listen patiently?"

"Well, yes." She giggled. "Or defend yourself—but not until I'm done telling you what you've done wrong."

"But no agreeing?"

"None at all."

"What if I feel bad for being so horrid and want to beg for forgiveness?"

She sighed and rolled over on her side again, burying her face within his comforting fur and changed the subject completely. "I've thought of a few names for you."

He chuckled. "Do they involve death threats?"

"You mean perhaps, Slain or Target?"

"Those would work, though perchance you should consider Clown or Moron."

Cecelia laughed. "No, no, no. I've thought of much better names."

"Oh, dear, do I want to hear them?"

He could feel her shrug against him. "I don't know. You may consider me silly, but I was thinking along the lines of Apollo, or Beau, or Calixto."

Alexander stopped breathing. It was a full minute before he could speak again in a ragged hushed tone. "But those names—they all mean handsome or beautiful."

"Yes, they do. It's why I chose them."

He had no idea in that moment a wolf could become choked up. How did he never see the splendor that was this girl before now? How had his life become so vain and foolish and reckless that he never stopped to see the great tower of strength she was? The wisdom and kindness of her heart completely undid him. Alexander had to blink several times, before he asked, "Why?"

She buried herself deeper against his side. "Because you are beautiful."

"No, I'm an ugly beast who has unwittingly ruined your trust and your life."

Cecelia took a deep breath. "You have ruined my trust and you are bordering on ruining my life. But, I cannot—I will not overlook the reasons why you chose to do what you did. And though I feel involving Prince Alexander and sharing my secrets with him has done much to make me want to strangle you, being here under the stars, next to my magical brook, I have to own that you are indeed the kindest and most gentle creature the good Lord has ever formed."

Humbled beyond measure the beast could only ask, "How did you ever draw such a conclusion? How can anyone look past their own hurt to see the good intentions behind the pain?"

"I do not understand what you ask? Doesn't everyone step back and see things from another's perspective?"

The prince shook his head and owned quite truthfully, "I did not until you taught me so. Until then I could only see my own haughtiness and prideful ugliness."

She wrapped her arm around his side, and settled her head higher upon his back. "Do you feel ugly?"

"Hideous, unsightly, revolting, repulsi—"

"But why?" She ran her hand across his side to soothe him. "You are honestly the most striking wolf I have ever met."

He closed his eyes. "Yes, for a wolf I will own that I am quite dashing. However, it is my soul I speak of, my inner peace with myself. I am not all I could be, not all I want to be, there is so much more to improve upon. So much more I must learn first."

"Mayhap, but we all have things we wish to improve upon." She sat up and scratched his ears. "Come on, no more sadness. Which name do you choose? Apollo, Beau, or Calixto?"

"None, Cecelia." He looked out toward the forest. "No matter how I try to perceive myself differently I will only ever be a monster."

"Please do not be so hard upon yourself."

"How can I not? I must live this horror every day as a reminder of who and what I truly am. I have hurt you, I have placed you in a worse predicament than before and I have no idea how to fix what damage I have done. How you can even speak to me as such is beyond more than I deserve."

"Shh…"

"No, Cecelia, you are kind and everything good in this world, while I am nothing but a dreadful beast."

"Listen to me. Listen closely to what I say to you, for it is the truth." She moved herself to be to where he could see her best, held his sweet head between her hands and simply said the most amazing words Prince Alexander had ever heard.

"You may be a beast, but you have more beauty in your heart than anyone I know."

# Chapter Eleven

FREDERICK COULD HAVE hurled, the scene before him was so disgusting. When his cousin had bounded down the stone palace steps outside with the large heart necklace swinging in his hand, right around dusk, Lord Bellemount knew without a doubt he was on his way to meet the girl. So, he did the only advisable thing to do at the moment, he followed him.

He'd already pursued him earlier that day, but the prince had merely wandered a few miles away from the castle to a little stream and found a rose which he had picked up and then meandered his way back to the palace.

Nothing exciting, nothing certainly to be concerned over, but this time, with the heart-shaped necklace, he was bound to be going to whatever girl he'd fallen in love with.

Frederick pushed off from his hiding spot and began trailing his cousin, which ended up being much harder than he anticipated.

Never had he expected his cousin to turn into a wolf before his eyes. But he did just that, about two hundred yards into the forest, just as darkness fell, the beast tore from within the prince's body and transformed him.

Frederick was scared out of his wits at first, especially of the ear-splitting howl that accompanied such an alteration. It was so loud and painful all Lord Bellemount could do was cover his ears and fall back against a tree.

And then the wolf was gone, tearing through the forest at a much faster rate than he could have imagined.

When Frederick got to the place where his cousin had changed, the necklace was nowhere to be found. Alexander had to have picked it up and taken it with him. At the rate he left, instead of falling to the ground in agony, meant the transformation was expected, this was something that was normal. Perhaps even a daily occurrence.

Prince Alexander had to have been halfway to the gel by now.

With hasty steps Frederick began to track the animal, just the same way he'd learned as a boy to track the hounds that had gone off to chase the fox during hunting season.

By the time he came upon them both, he was tired and weary and seething mad. His feet were burning within his boots and he'd wandered over two hours down dead ends and useless tracks until he finally stumbled upon them. It was clearly obvious his cousin had been over every square inch of the land as a wolf, his tracks were everywhere.

So when he overheard her speaking and then quieted his breathing enough to determine where the sound was coming from, it was only a matter of a few steps to his left, following the path of the stream that led him to the little clearing that held them both. The exact same place Alexander had been earlier and collected the flower.

This was their meeting spot. The rose must have been some sort of sign to meet her.

She was indeed very pretty, but even Lord Bellemount did not expect Miss Hammerstein-Smythe to be the object of his cousin's desires. He knew his tastes and knew his feelings about the girl. So why her? Why now after all this time was it she who captured his heart?

And capture it she did.

Frederick watched them for a few minutes, enough to see the imaginary glow that seemed to come from them both. But when she walked in front of the beast and held his wolfly face in her hands and uttered that nonsense about Alexander's inner beauty, Frederick knew he was in danger.

No man, no matter how much he claimed otherwise, could resist an attractive woman telling him his worst fears were for naught, and she truly believed he was worth more than he supposed.

There were several confusing questions to this riddle that would only be solved by staying a bit longer and gleaning as much information as possible. Did Miss Hammerstein-Smythe know who the wolf was? If she did, how could she tolerate it? Had not his cousin been despicable toward her

for years? And if she did not know he was
the prince, then how could she be so calm and
cheerful around a wolf?

Lord Bellemount silently sat down against
a tree, hidden behind bushes that allowed
enough space between them to see and hear
what was going on.

"Cecelia?"

"Yes?" She looked down into the wolf's
gaze and gently rubbed above his left eyebrow.

"How does a man win your affection? I'm
sure you have many men vying for you."

She laughed. "Have you forgotten my
misfortunes? The ones that forced you to
reveal all to Prince Alexander on my behalf?"
She looked away and briefly winced. "There
aren't many men; there isn't even one thanks
to Lord Willington's disapproval of me."

"Well, there is one, but you do not
approve of him."

She glanced back. "Who? Prince
Alexander?"

"Yes."

She shook her head and grinned, dropping

her hands. "But he does not count."

"You don't consider him man enough? Is it because of his past actions toward you?—he told me everything." Alexander quickly added.

"Yes, perhaps. His actions do weigh heavily on my mind, but that is not what I am thinking of now—it has nothing to do with our history."

"Then what?"

"Well, he was at my home because you asked him to go. He was not there because he cares for me. And even though he feels he is doing good by seeming to court me publicly, there can only be harm that comes of it." She shifted her weight and leaned against one arm, with her legs tucked under her. "For eventually he will leave me, and then what will the villagers say to that? To be scorned by one man is bad enough, but to be seen as a mad game of the prince's to play..." Her voice softened and trailed away.

He should be celebrating her good sense and using this as his excuse to disentangle the prince from the picture, but he could not help but ask, "Do you like him?"

Cecelia softly gasped. "I—I don't know.

I am trying so hard to stay detached and see him as a new friend, to get to know this person that he has appeared to become."

"Do you think you could one day?"

"Like him?" she asked, stalling.

Alexander's heart was racing. "Yes."

After a few moments she said, "I think I need to learn to trust him first." When the wolf did not speak again, she added, "I do trust that he means well, and I do trust that he has changed. Anyone can see that he has changed; there is a new inner strength that wasn't there before. He's calmer and happier now. But, I'm not sure he will stay this way."

He knew he should allow this to be the time when he took control of the situation and told her he would tell the prince to leave her in peace and allow that to be that, but when he opened his mouth to speak, he was shocked to hear himself ask, "What would you like me to tell him?" giving Cecelia the reins to decide the next course of action.

To leave me alone. To never come back. To find something or someone else to pester and harass and pretend to be in love with. "I do not know," she whispered.

Alexander gulped and tried to control his heart. Nothing had ever meant more to him than the acceptance and forgiveness of a woman he loved greater than life itself. "Cecelia, do you think you could learn to completely trust and like him as time moves forward? And if he proves himself, do you think he could become something special to you?"

"Yes." Cecelia gasped again. "No, I meant no. Of course not!" She shook her head and fidgeted with her gown. "This is nonsense. None of this matters. He will never see me as more than a village girl and I will never fully trust anyone again."

"Never?"

His gaze captured hers and held it for quite some time, before she answered truthfully, "I would give anything to learn to trust again, to know I am truly loved. Anything. But there are days I feel I will never become more than a silly girl in anyone's eyes."

"He loves you."

"What did you say?" Cecelia could hardly hear a word over the pounding of her heart.

"I—I said," Alexander frantically searched his mind. "I have something for you."

"Oh." Her face fell. "I thought you had said something else."

"What did you think I had said?"

She waved her hand. "Oh, nothing. Something silly that made no sense anyway." She quickly changed the subject. "So what did you bring this time? Another poem?"

"Remember I mentioned earlier it wasn't something you'd enjoy hitting me with as much as you would a book."

She laughed. "Yes, I remember."

"Well, if you look underneath that patch of clover over there you'll find it." He nodded his head, indicating where the gift was.

Cecelia brushed aside the clover. "Good heavens! It's stunning." She very gently picked the necklace up. "Are you sure you meant this for me?"

"Positively sure."

"Oh, I—I don't know what to say." She fingered the delicate gold rose that wrapped around the large red heart. I've never seen something more perfect in all of my life."

"Put it on, please."

She carefully clasped the gold chain around her neck and marveled at the weight of the heart as it lay against her chest. It was truly the most expensive and beautiful gift she'd ever been given. "What did I do to deserve such a token?"

He shrugged and then said, "It's an apology of sorts for betraying your trust in me."

Cecelia chuckled. "If this is an apology, I wonder what type of jewelry you'd give to someone you were professing your love to!"

He grinned and raised an eyebrow. "Oh, well, now—if I was actually professing my love, you could guarantee it would be something much grander than that."

"Should I be concerned where it is you're getting such beautiful things from?" she taunted.

"Good heavens, woman, I'm not stealing them. I have a home, you know."

She was intrigued, having never thought of him in a house before. "You do?"

"Well, of course I do." He sat fully up and teasingly looked down his nose at her with the accent of a Northerner. "How else do you think I'm so cultured and refined?"

Cecelia laughed. "And handsome, you forgot handsome."

"Well, that goes without saying."

She smiled as she looked him over. He was an incredibly beautiful wolf. "Can I call you Apollo?"

"You do know he was an inexcusable womanizer, don't you? At least that's what the legends of the Greek gods say."

"It doesn't matter. I like it best, and I think it is a perfect name for you. Besides, a name is just a name. Because one man acting as such doesn't hold true that another with the same name would. No, my dear beast, you shall be called Apollo."

He grinned. "And why does it matter so much if you call me anything at all?"

"Why? So I can thank you properly before I leave, of course. I must head home soon, or I may be missed." Cecelia raised herself up on her knees until they were nose to nose. "Thank you, Apollo. Thank you for everything." And then she leaned up a fraction of a bit more, tilted his head down and kissed him right upon the forehead.

Alexander's heart melted.

Frederick, however, was going to be sick to his stomach.

a long debate over the matter, when his nose caught a familiar smell to his left.

Frederick!

Whipping his head in that direction, he flicked his ears, determined to find the cause of such an odd occurrence. If it was truly his cousin, then what was he doing out here in the woods at this time of night?

He caught the faint sound of rustling and then the distinct smell of fear began to take its place burning its way through his senses.

Lord Bellemount was here!

Alexander's sharp eyes could make out enough of his form through the bushes across the way to know exactly where the coward was hiding. What should he do? The prince's first instinct was to ferret the weasel out and eat him for a midnight snack.

However, since his cousin was in no doubt terrified at the moment and not stupid enough to flee, he figured he had some time to weigh his options. The beast walked forward and lied down on the forest floor about twenty feet from the culprit and decided to make sure Frederick's anxiety levels rose a few more notches.

And there they went.

He chuckled as the fear smell intensified. As far as the wolf was concerned, he had all the time in the world to decide what to do about his devious heir. It was obvious he knew his secret, as well as what girl he was in love with. But what was his cousin planning to do with such information now that he knew it? This was the real question and something that would need some time to mull over, for if Alexander had learned anything over the past five or six months, it was that he should never make a rash decision simply based in anger, or he would live to regret it.

He had to be smart. He had to consider all of his options.

But what? And how? He began nuzzling his paw as if he were not there guarding Frederick and instead merely enjoying the nice night air. He could walk away and pretend as though he did not know his cousin knew as much as he did, hoping to follow and watch him on his own, when he had a better idea of the consequences.

Or he could pounce upon him now and demand answers. Alexander smiled, then

grimaced. Yet, that may not be the wisest course of action—though definitely the most satisfying—it would do nothing but guarantee Lord Bellemount's anger later. He could not kill him on just suspicion alone. If he did that, he'd be no better than the monster he was months ago.

There was one person to consider during all of this, and that was Cecelia. Her life, her happiness, her fragile existence right now was more important than anything at all. It was no secret her being was secure and happier with him than without. She needed him as much as he needed her.

The issue with Frederick would have to be handled delicately so as not to disrupt the slight bond beginning to form between them. But, Alexander would make sure his cousin rued the day he decided to ever lay a hand on Miss Hammerstein-Smythe, monster or not, he'd kill him.

IT WAS SEVERAL minutes of anxious terror and waiting to see if he had been caught or not before Lord Bellemount was finally able

to let out a sigh of relief and allow his heart to
stop racing. He peeked out of the bushes and
watched as his cousin's wolf form walk briskly
away.

That was close! Too close.

He was sure Alexander had spotted him,
but he must have heard something beyond the
place where he was hiding instead. Talk about
fright. Frederick had never seen his cousin
look so intimidating before. It was downright
disconcerting to see him appear like a large
forest beast. But then to see him court the gel
as an animal was unthinkable!

He smirked. The dim-witted girl did not
even know who she was talking to. That fact
alone had to have been the most ironic notion
there was. Simply laughable! How would
Miss Hammerstein-Smythe feel if she knew
her secret beau was in fact the prince she had
always detested?

Frederick sneered in glee. Perhaps he
should toy a bit with this concept and see what
humorous findings he could come up with.
Imagine the spoke in his cousin's wheel if all
were to be revealed? For that matter, what
would the villagers say to such a finding?

Their dear sweet princely hero turned into a ravenous, beastly wolf at night.

My, my, my…the world around Lord Bellemount became a whole lot brighter in an instant.

It would seem he had some planning to do.

CECELIA STRETCHED AND sighed as she awoke the next morning. The sunlight gloriously trickled through the window on shimmery dust trails, making it appear as if glitter were delicately dancing all around her.

Today was going to be a perfect day.

Giggling, she leapt from the bed and quickly donned a pretty white gown with blue and green trimmings. Then she slipped the necklace on and marveled once again at the weight of the thing. The dark maroon color of the red was simply beautiful against the white of her dress. She tucked the heart inside her filigreed-laced bodice, and turned from side to side within the looking glass, making sure it remained hidden from view. If her mother saw it, she'd no doubt conclude it came from none other than the prince himself and then she'd never hear the end of it.

No, some things were better kept to herself for a short time longer.

Cecelia had no idea why she had a sudden urge to be dressed and out of the house so quickly, but after hurrying through breakfast and her usual morning chat with Sanford, she allowed her maid to hastily pin her hair up in a quick bun, and securing her bonnet atop her head, she was out the back door before anyone had realized she'd gone.

It was a bright warm day, full of sunshine and hope, and no need for her pelisse. She wandered through her mother's rose garden deciding on a beautiful white rose to leave for Apollo, before scurrying down the path to her brook.

She had a lot to think about and many conversations to go over from the past few days. There was definitely a change, some sort of excitement or buzz forming within her soul, and she needed to sort it out before she understood what was happening to her.

Cecelia had wondered if she'd ever feel this way again, and yet here she was more

giddy and happy than she'd been in weeks.
If only she could put her finger on the exact
cause, it would prove to be much more helpful.
Why now the sudden change of energy and
liveliness that seemed to spring from her?
Why all the excitement? And who was it that
was causing such a disruption to her daily
oddities and notions?

With the way her heart had begun to race
at the thought it was someone, rather than
something, worried her a bit. Because who
had she met, other than the prince, the last few
days? And she surely wouldn't have allowed
herself the silliness of falling in love with him,
just because he was kind enough to pay her a
visit.

No, it had to be something else disrupting
her altogether. Perhaps the wolf had a bit to
do with it? It was no surprise he had definitely
enhanced her joy and life altogether, but
the fluttering within her was something she
couldn't quite place. There was a reason she
was feeling this way, and definitely the brook
was the only spot where she was bound to
have the freedom and solitude to discover the
answers.

As she came upon the little stream, however, she was surprised to see she was not alone. In fact, if she didn't know better, it would seem as if the prince's cousin, Lord Bellemount was sitting in the exact spot her beast liked to sit.

# Chapter Thirteen

JUST AS SHE was about to retrace her steps and come again later, Lord Bellemount called out to her.

"Miss Hammerstein-Smythe, a word, if you please?"

Cecelia halted, her fingers tightened around the prickly stem of the rose she was carrying. The last thing she wanted to do was speak with the arrogant Lord, but found propriety dictated she at least be civil. Dipping into a short curtsy, she answered, "I am unchaperoned at the moment, so should not stay. Forgive me."

She would've turned then, but he stood

up and crossed the stream as he spoke. "Wait. Just a few moments of your time, nothing more."

She stepped back a few paces to keep some distance between them. It would seem it was no accident that she stumbled upon the man; it was as if he were waiting for her. Cecelia almost dreaded what it was he wished to speak to her about. The only connection she could find of his appearance, the only other person who knew of this particular spot was the prince himself, which would indicate he told him about her.

Cecelia's worst thoughts became reality when within the next breath Lord Bellemount unleashed his nastiness. Having had plenty of time over the course of the following evening during his walk home to devise this, he thought it only expedient he put his course of action into plan immediately. So as soon as he'd woken that morning, he had dressed and headed right for this little brook. Knowing if his calculations were correct, the gel would be approaching this place sometime in the morning to deliver her rose.

When he saw her bounding down the

path not some twenty minutes later with the coveted flower in her hand, he knew without a doubt this was going to be a very pleasant day. Without further ado, he grinned and complimented her. "My dear Miss Hammerstein-Smythe, first may I say indeed that my cousin has been utterly remiss in his exclamations of your charm and beauty of late." He swept into a grand bow, his hand going from head to toe, taking in all of her person. "Why, look at you! The perfect picture of grace, and yet you would think by the way Alexander was describing you just yesterday, I was expecting something quite the opposite."

Her heart sank and her hand twitched slightly under the pressure of the rose thorns pressed into her palm. "The opposite?"

"Well, we did have a good laugh at your misfortunes, at your expense, of course."

"My misfortunes."

"Yes, well, do not take it to heart, my cousin and I simply cannot help teasing and mocking those we come in contact with. It is our favorite pastime, and something we've always done." He shrugged. "But we do it to everyone, and so therefore it is only fair we mention you from time to time."

"I see." She swallowed and asked, "And what was it he told you of?" She took a step forward, her fingers unconsciously tearing at the petals. "Did he mention he was at my home yesterday and why?" Her voice rose. "Did he also tell you of Lord Willington and of the villagers as well?"

Frederick had no idea to what she was referring, but did not let his smirk waver one iota as he answered, "What else would we have mocked so willingly?"

Cecelia tore the crushed rose from its stem and threw them both upon the ground, allowing the petals to float haphazardly around her feet. "You two may believe you have the right to mock those beneath you, and laugh and smirk at who you will, but you do not." She took another pace forward and then another, forcing Lord Bellemount to retreat a half step. "If you think either of you will get away with such callous treatment of those of your kingdom, then mark my words, you won't."

"But—" He'd meant to be the victor in

this conversation; he had expected her to be grateful for the knowledge the prince had betrayed her. He'd hoped to guarantee she would hate his cousin so much, he then could reveal the final blow that Alexander was her precious beast and watch her crumble. Watch her go mad from the duplicity of both.

"No! There is no reason for such juvenile behavior from either of you." She continued to walk forward, forcing him back, until he slipped on the small grassy slope of the brook and sunk one boot into the water.

"You misunderstand!" He grappled to try and make sense at the tyrant girl before him, his other boot slipping into the stream as well. Where had this anger come from? "You must see that I came here to warn you, and distinguish for myself if you were as dreadful as he painted you. And you're not! Not at all!" Frederick grimaced as he felt the cold water trickle through his boots and slosh against his feet. You're much, much worse.

Cecelia stepped forward until they were face to face. "Lord Bellemount, you may tell Prince Alexander that I find him the most despicable human being I've ever had the misfortune of meeting, and if I ever see you or him again, it will be too soon!"

She had not meant to, but her own reactions and anger took over to the point where before she knew what she was about, Cecelia had quite successfully shoved the prince's heir by the shoulders to land in a heap upon his bottom in the wet grass, his feet still drenched in the chilly water. "Good day!" she exclaimed in agitation, before turning upon her heel and marching back home.

She let out several frustrated howls and very unladylike grunts and groans, kicking a number of very harmless stones and daises out of her way as she stormed back to the house and into her bedroom. Once there, she flung her bonnet off and just before she threw it against the wall, she checked herself, remembering she liked this particular hat and would hate to see it smashed because the prince was an inconceivable pig. Instead, she allowed it to bounce on the bench in front of her bed.

Ooh! The audacity of the man! She knew it. She knew he had not changed! And yet, almost, almost she had believed him. It was a close call on her part, but may she forever keep this day as a reminder that some people will never alter who they truly are.

With a sigh, Cecelia sat down upon her bed. What sort of ill-fated folly drove all of this to her door anyway? Could she perhaps have just one day of peace and happiness? Just one, where she knew the world was good and the hope she'd always carried would be worth the anguish it brought when it began to fade…

She closed her eyes and laid down, curling against her pillow and pulling her knees up upon the duvet. Her heart was wounded more than she cared to admit. The shame of imagining the glee the two men—no, boys—found at her expense was agonizing. What was the point in hope anyway, when all she ever faced was mockery and chastisement?

One fragile tear made its way down her nose, splattering upon her other cheek, and continued to forge a trail until it collided with her pillow and sank into its downy relief. Soon a stream of tears followed and Cecelia Hammerstein-Smythe cried herself to sleep in the only sanctuary she had left—her room.

ALEXANDER STRETCHED AND yawned out the weariness of his body. This forever changing night and day was beginning to take its toll upon his muscles. It seemed each morning found a new array of aches and pains he didn't perceive possible to find upon his person.

Glancing out the window he cursed his even later night than usual. It was clearly the afternoon. What time was it anyway? His pocket fob was on the dresser across the room, but if he had to take a guess he'd assume it was nearly two, which meant already half of his day as a man was gone.

With a groan he flung off the covers and climbed out of bed. Padding across the large room, he rang for his valet and began to pour the water for himself into his washbasin. Soon with the help of his valet, he was shaved, dressed, and looking every inch a dignified prince again.

He'd decided early this morning, just before the sun had risen, that he would risk the

villager's gossip, his cousin, and the wrath of
Miss Hammerstein-Smythe, and continue to
see Cecelia. He had to. His own pride would
not allow her to merely become friends with
a beast. For some reason, he felt he needed to
prove to himself he could attain the impossible
and get the gel to fall for her enemy as well.
To see that he truly had transformed before her
eyes, and to hopefully make up for the lack
of his charms he'd subjected her to all those
times earlier.

He had never met a more perfect girl in
all his days, and he could not stay away. No
matter how foolish or dangerous it proved to
them both, he allowed the impractical to rule
his mind and for once in his life relish in as
much opportunity as he could in the delightful
company of Miss Hammerstein-Smythe.

Besides, he thought with an erratic beating
of justification in his heart, how better to keep
tabs on Frederick than to spend as much time
as possible with her?

It was with great eagerness and a bouquet
of freshly cut multi-colored tulips, that
Alexander ordered Sterling to be brought
round from the stables and rode off to meet the

girl who'd captured his soul.

## Chapter Fourteen

CECELIA OPENED HER eyes to a loud
pounding upon her door. Another second
brought her mother barging into the room
in an ornate dress of violet satin and silver
trimmings. "Why in the world do you sleep in
the middle of the afternoon?" She rushed to
the bed. "Get up! Get up! Prince Alexander
is here to see you."

When Cecelia stirred and sat up, her
mother gasped.

"Are you not feeling well?" She placed
a warm palm against her daughter's flushed
cheek. "Well, you are not on fire at least. But
good heavens, child, I've never seen you look

so ill before. What has happened?"

"Nothing has happened worth speaking of." She groaned and got down from the bed, making her way to the looking glass all the while her mother droned on about how horrid she looked. But it wasn't until she saw the pathetic girl looking back at her with swollen eyes, red nose, and pale features, that Cecelia realized how truly awful she appeared. In fact, she had never looked worse. Yanking a hand through the frazzled curls escaping her bun, she turned to her mother and said simply, "Good." It was the perfect complexion for slaying a prince.

"Good? What do you mean by saying such a thing to me?" When her daughter did not answer she continued, "What is good? There can be nothing good about you at the moment, especially when taking your appearance into consideration."

Ignoring her mother, Cecelia splashed some water on her face from the washbasin on her dresser and pulled the rest of the pins from her hair, letting them cascade down her back in a plethora of riotous curls before plainly stating, "Personally, I do not give a fig for what the prince thinks of my looks at the moment."

"I beg your pardon?" Her mother's hand flew to her chest.

Cecelia sighed and crossed the room. While opening the door she asked, "Where is he? In the parlor?"

"Cecelia Josephine Hammerstein-Smythe, if you step one foot out that door, in such disarray, I shall flog you!"

"I'll get the crop," was her only answer as she stepped into the hallway.

She was halfway down the stairs before her mother made it to the top of the steps and hissed, "Cecelia, do not do it! Do not let him see you this way! Think of the scandal!"

"Oh, I promise you, I can think of nothing else," she mumbled under her breath as she took the remainder of the stairs at a faster pace. When she burst into the parlor, the prince wasn't the only one to jump. Sanford took one look at her countenance and quickly mumbled something about fetching a footman and was gone, the door swinging closed behind him.

They were all alone.

"Miss Hammerstein-Smythe, is there anything wrong?" Alexander asked tentatively, his eyes taking in her long tresses, "You seem out of sorts."

She walked up to him, choosing not to satisfy him with an answer to that question, she said, "You have one minute to collect your hat and coat and then you will leave."

"Leave?"

"Now." She refused to look at him, focusing on a point just over her his left shoulder instead.

Alexander's gaze traced her wan features, carefully searching them for answers. He had never seen her so distressed, so determined, so...so callused. And yet, though she looked wretched—as if betrayed and beaten down by an unthinkable foe—she still was the most beautiful girl he had ever seen. "How have I harmed you, my dear? Will you please tell me? It is I who has harmed you, is it not? What can I do to make it better?" he asked quietly.

Startled, her eyes flew to his and she was surprised to see compassion and contrition within their depths. It made her feel a loss of balance within herself, and she wasn't quite sure what to say. He'd done the most despicable, horrid type of mockery, and yet here he was standing before her looking as though he would die before uttering a false word in her name.

Who was this man standing her? Was he the snobbish prince, or the kindhearted gentleman? He plainly could not be both.

While her guard was slipping, he stepped forward and placed a hand on her shoulder, his knuckles brushing against her hair. "My dear, whatever it is I have done or said, or have not done or said, or whatever I have harmed you with…" he leaned forward, trying to comfort in any way possible. His eyes closed as his mouth moved along her brow and he continued whispering, "…whatever it is that has put such hallowed hopeless looks upon your face, I am sorry. Terribly, dreadfully sorry."

Her lashes fluttered, her senses were in complete disarray taking in the smell of his shaving soap and the bridge of her nose caressing his smooth jaw. She had never stood so close to a man before for any extended amount of time.

When his lips stilled and pressed against her forehead, leaving a kiss there, a small breath escaped at the fissured sparks that zinged down her neck and to the shoulder he was holding. Her hand reached up and clung to his suit coat as her lips unconsciously searched and reached for his.

Alexander was more than willing to oblige, and pressed his mouth to hers savoring the perfect softness beneath his. When she let out a little groan, he swept her up completely in his arms and continued the kiss, marveling at her willingness to accept him.

Cecelia had no thought recollection in that moment, nothing to recall herself to her true outlook of him; only the moment of abandoned feelings existed. She'd never before behaved so recklessly, but could not help herself; nothing had ever felt more right in her life. She needed the prince to want her, to care for her, to understand her, to love her.

To love her.

She gasped and broke free, moving several steps away from him—her breath coming in great humiliating gulps. It took a moment to apprehend he was having just as much difficultly in learning to breathe again as she.

Cecelia frowned slightly and then chuckled in spite of herself. "I fear we may have a problem."

"Do you believe so?" he asked, still not fully himself.

"Well, if this kissing is a bit to go by, then yes, I believe we clearly have a problem."

"And what is that?" he asked taking a step closer.

She tugged on a long lock of black hair and began wrapping it around her finger. "Can you not tell for yourself?"

"No." He took another step closer. "Enlighten me."

She glanced away quickly and then met his eyes again. "I feel as though I could strangle you, and yet, for some reason I must be near you when you are around." She was about to go on and explain why she wanted to strangle him and why she felt so wretched and all sorts of other inklings and rememberings of grievances passed through her mind to tell him, but just as she was ready to continue on,

Prince Alexander took another couple of steps and knelt down before her.

He placed her hands in his and while looking up with great earnestness said, "My dear Miss Hammerstein-Smythe, it would do me the greatest honor if you would consent to be my wife."

His game—this mockery—had gone too far, her heart hardened and cooled instantly.

Cecelia pulled her hands away. She could forgive him for scorning her as he always had, and his jesting. She could forgive him for his great pretending of kindness and sweet disposition when he was in front of her. She could even forgive him for what he was doing to try and save her from her own folly and the gossips surrounding her mistakes, no matter how much pleasure he derived of it later. However, she simply, positively could not tolerate him professing his undying love and need to make her his.

If there were ever a time when Prince Alexander had the upper hand, it was now. But she plainly could not allow such nonsense to even enter her mind. Not when she could imagine the great laugh he and Lord

Bellemount would have at her expense in just a few hours from then.

No, if there was one thing she had always despised it was someone who was so arrogant they did not give a thought to another's wellbeing over their own. Prince Alexander, though he may look sweet and acted friendly, was nothing different than he always had been. She had known him long enough to realize he was never going to change either.

Her jaw tightened and she raised her chin. "Please leave as soon as possible."

His mouth opened and an expression of hurt flashed across his features. "Why? What have I done?"

She would not be taken in by his false sincerity. "Nothing more than I have come to expect."

He stood, his eyes scanning her face and reached for her hands again, but she turned her back on him. "Why won't you tell me?"

Crossing her arms, she could not face him. "Because it does not matter."

He looked around the empty room, hopeless on how to reach her. It was there his eyes rested on the bouquet of tulips he'd brought from the hothouse garden; its pretty pink ribbon dangling off the ornamental table placed next to the high-backed chair he'd been sitting upon.

Collecting the joyful flowers, he stepped forward and gingerly placed a hand on her left shoulder while his arm reached around the right and presented them to her. "It may not matter to you, but it most certainly matters to me. Nothing has ever mattered more to me. If you could but see what I truly feel for you, I promise I would love you forever."

The deep voice near her ear, the hand gently squeezing her shoulder, the smell of the sweet flowers, and the sensation of him so near her nearly had her forgetting for a moment how horrid the situation was. For a few seconds she closed her eyes and imagined what it would be like to truly be cared for by such a man. He gave such a distinct impression of security and strength and kindness as to undo all of her senses completely. She had forgotten how to breathe, how to think, how to care about the consequences of acceptance of such actions.

In fact, Miss Cecelia Hammerstein-

Smythe, for just a few moments, allowed all
the imaginings of such glorious and happy
thoughts to enter her mind, she'd forgotten
completely that she was fraternizing with the
enemy.

But, oh, what splendid thoughts they
were! If he were truly to be trusted! If a man,
as he professed to be, actually existed there
would be no doubt as to where her affection
would lie. None at all.

No, it would be him who would have to
run from her, because she would never ever let
a man like what Prince Alexander pretended to
be escape.

# Chapter Fifteen

TEARS FORMED IN Cecelia's eyes as she turned fully in his strong arms—arms that immediately wrapped all the way around her. There was gentleness in her tone as she glanced up and whispered, "Please, leave, please."

She was obviously distraught; he took note of the wetness of her gaze as well as the wobble in her voice. Silently sighing, he gave in. He could not deny her anything when she was in such a state. "If you wish it, I will leave you."

Alexander watched as she closed her eyes briefly and allowed her head to fold into his shoulder, her glorious hair tickling his nose as she did so. He held her for a few moments before she mumbled into his coat, "I believe it would be best."

"Perhaps." His chin rubbed along the black silky curls beneath it. He would have to press her as the wolf and find out what it was she wouldn't tell him.

She snuggled in closer, her other hand playing with the smooth fabric of his tied cravat. "You are simply the most horrid man in the world. I cannot stand the sight of you."

"I know." He nodded and placed a kiss at the top of her head.

"Despicable human being, I never want to see you again," she mumbled into his coat.

Alexander's right hand clutching the bouquet shifted to allow his left to begin trailing slowly over her back. "I will leave immediately," he agreed, not moving one inch.

She melted into him at the warmth of his caress. "And you'll never see me again?"

"Never. I wouldn't dream of seeing you again."

She looked up. "Truly?"

"Truly."

She pulled back slightly to see him more fully. "Good."

"Good," he repeated, his eyes twinkling. "Can I kiss you once more, before I leave and never see you again?"

"I will most likely strangle you once you're done."

He grinned. "Put me out of my misery?"

She nodded. "Mm-hm."

Alexander leaned forward and watched as her eyes drifted shut. His grin deepened. She may despise him, but there was no doubt in his mind that Miss Hammerstein-Smythe was besotted. Knowing the best way to guarantee he'd see her again was to leave her unsure of his intentions, he allowed his mouth to hover just above hers and then he whispered, "I better not. It would be cruel to tease you in such a way, especially with how much you dislike me at the moment; it would only create a longing for more."

She pulled out of his arms and glared.

The prince covered a smile with a low bow. When he came up, he took one of her hands and placed the tulips in her palm. "Good day, my fair lady." He chuckled then, he could not help himself. "I am sure I will never see you again." With that, he turned on his heel and left, leaving a very perplexed Miss Hammerstein-Smythe in his wake.

PRINCE ALEXANDER LEFT via the front door, but after fetching Sterling, he decided to make his way down to the brook and see if Cecelia had already left a rose for the wolf. Slipping off the horse's back as he approached, his eyes took in the scene in front of him.

White rose petals were strewn everywhere, the twisted stem crushed and left bereft of beauty upon the ground where he stood.

What had happened?

He bent down and examined the petals. It was obvious they had been plucked from their stem and crushed and bruised within a hand before being scattered. Concern marred his brow as he imagined the pretty girl coming here with her rose, and then something occurring to make her so distraught she had destroyed the flower completely. Perhaps something concerning himself or the beast?

And yet, when he found her she did not say one word about the wolf. No, her anger was directed solely toward him. Had it been Apollo she was upset with she would have had no problem stating the fact.

It was as he was examining the ground closer he noticed a large boot print stuck in the softened soil near the brook.

Frederick had been here.

Alexander cursed under his breath. How did he not see this coming?

Examining the crushed foliage around the area, he realized she was most decidedly not happy with Lord Bellemount as well. It looked like she'd flattened him somehow. Alexander smiled. Good girl, was his thought before sobering to the reality his cousin had already been afoot doing considerably more damage than he'd thought capable in less than twenty-four hours.

Rising again, Alexander sighed. It would seem it was time to pay his wayward heir a visit. Enough was enough. And frankly, any man who deemed it necessary to upset his Cecelia would need to answer to him first.

Prince Alexander rode all over the

countryside and could not find his cousin.
He stopped in at Lord Bellemount's stately
manor upon the ridge, and demanded answers
there of his staff and sisters, neither of whom
claimed to have any recollection of where
he has. After storming the whole house, he
himself had to realize they were speaking the
truth. Frederick was not there.

After hours of scouring the land, he came
home a few minutes before nightfall hungry
and empty-handed and more determined than
ever to find the man.

The moment the order was dispatched,
his servants began to search through his own
gardens and palace grounds as well as any
other properties he owned. He would find
Frederick and he would get to the bottom of
this, this evening, or heads would roll.

Climbing the stairs two at a time, his mind
raced through way too many possibilities to
guarantee rationality. What had happened?
What had he said? Did she know he was
Apollo?

No, she couldn't have. He knew her well
enough to know that would have been her first
accusation the second she had burst into the

parlor.

What did he say to her?! Alexander was going mad and he only had a few minutes before the moon came out to shovel some food in his mouth and get ready for his meeting with her later that night. That is, if she was still willing to meet him.

He was not certain, but he could not help but try and show up nevertheless. Cecelia was going to need a friend, if anything else, she needed his strength. He had to be there for her. And she clearly needed protection from his cousin.

"Arrgh!" the wolf roared in pain and frustration as he made his way from the castle property into the surrounding land a few minutes later—the servants still searching through the grounds, jumped at the sound but did not stop their search to find the cause of it.

When he got to the brook, he paced up and down the area for a while before lying down and attempting to calm his mind. It was difficult with the petals strewn everywhere, but he succeeded, just. He would discover what had happened if she came, and then he would find and annihilate the man responsible.

An hour or so later brought Cecelia down the path to the little stream. She did not realize until right before she got there that she had no recollection of placing the rose upon the stone. In fact, she wasn't quite sure what had become of the flower after speaking with the prince's cousin. As she approached however, she was welcomed by the sight of petals strewn along the path, where the gentle breeze had pulled them up the short hill to greet her. The closer she came, the more petals she found, and her heart sank briefly at the thought of the beast's reaction to such a display from her. But before she could form any thoughts of his despising her and never coming again, she met Apollo's eyes across the water.

"You're here." Relief wound its way through her body, bringing a rich glow of warmth to settle over her heart. She immediately crossed the brook and sat down snuggling herself against him. "I have missed you so much," she whispered into his soft fur, her arm wrapped around his back.

Alexander's own heart warmed, another layer of its cold exterior cracked and crumbled within him. How could one girl do so much for his peace of mind, his character, and his happiness in such a short time? He could not deny his love for her, he never would. "I have missed you too," he answered, softly. "I have been concerned about you. Prince Alexander mentioned that you—"

"Ugh," she groaned quietly before raising her head and placing it upon his back. "Please do not speak his name tonight. I realize he has most likely told you of when he met with me earlier, but I came to see you, my dear Apollo, not hear about that perplexing man."

"Is he really awful?"

"Yes, and more."

"And more?" the wolf raised his head, and turned to catch a glimpse of her. "What has he done to upset you?"

She let out a deep breath and began to smooth the hair along his ears and jaw, causing tingles to spring to life with every follicle that was disrupted by the action. The beast was in heaven.

"Nothing much. The prince was playing

true to character, and I was silly enough to believe he had changed."

"Are you sure he has not changed? I could have sworn he seemed much different altogether lately."

"No."

She shook her head and began to scratch behind his ears, Apollo grunted in appreciation, his eyes closing. Cecelia chuckled. "Do you like that then?"

He could not answer; complete and utter bliss had overwhelmed him.

"I believe you do." She giggled again and began to use two hands.

The wolf turned to putty. Honestly, he'd give the adorable creature anything she wanted to feel this wonderful again.

After few moments of silence she asked, "Apollo?"

He cleared his throat, hoping to revive his vocal cords. "Yes?"

"I know I said I did not want to talk about him, but do you think the prince loves me?"

## Chapter Sixteen

ALEXANDER'S TAIL TWITCHED, he wasn't sure where Cecelia was going with the conversation. "Why?" he asked instead, hedging for some time.

Her hands stilled and paused before saying, "Because his actions claim to be very genuine, but the accounts I hear and know of him are completely the opposite."

"Has he told you he loved you?"

She turned over and looked up at the forest canopy and trickling moonlight above her, nestling into his warmth. "He has definitely alluded to it. Though Lord Bellemount said—oh…" her voice trailed off.

Apollo moved his back to nudge her when she remained silent. "What did Lord Bellemount say?"

She grumbled a bit before asking, "You won't be satisfied until I answer that question, will you?"

"I will more than likely hound you all evening until you open up and explain yourself. If the prince's cousin has told you anything, my dear, let me assure you—the man is a wastrel and a fop and deserves to be given as much credit as milksop weed."

She laughed. "Even if it is the truth?"

Alexander wished his eyes could have rolled right then. "Believe me, if it is the truth, which I highly doubt, then the chances of it being grossly exaggerated are great indeed. He is not a man to be universally trusted."

There was a long moment of silence before she answered quietly, "He came here this morning to see if the account of what Prince Alexander had said about me was false. He said they'd laughed tremendously at my expense and"—she took a deep breath—"and, Lord Bellemount believed the prince had been exaggerating and he found me much more enjoyable and pretty than his cousin did. Or something like that."

Apollo's tail begun to thump wildly. "Did he now?"

"At any rate, I apprehended this morning that the prince had not changed much at all, like I'd begun to believe."

"Cecelia," the wolf's deep voice pierced her, "Did his words harm you?"

"Not terribly noticeable—"

"Cecelia."

"Yes. Yes, they did—they wounded me more than I care to admit."

"Why?"

"Why?" She sat up. "Because he had said they mocked me and laughed at me and—"

"I know the lies he spewed, what I want to understand is why it hurt you so much."

She was silent for a while before answering, "Because I thought he was different. Because I thought—I had hoped—I could rely on him, but I couldn't."

"Do you love him?" Alexander held his breath, not sure what answer he wanted to hear more. One would guarantee the foolish prince had won her heart, and the other would guarantee he still had a chance to break this spell.

Cecelia straightened her gown and tucked her legs underneath her. "I don't know." She tested the answer over seriously in her mind before declaring, "No. I don't believe so. I cannot love someone I do not trust."

His breathing quickened as his heart raced. "Do you trust me?"

She turned and met his eyes. "Definitely. Did you not know that?"

"I wasn't sure." He glanced away.

A surprise chuckle escaped from her lips. "Of course I trust you. I would not be out here in the dark, to meet some strange dangerous beast, unless I did."

He grinned a wolfly grin and raised an eyebrow. "I think you make a legitimate point there."

"I would hope so!" She giggled and found a tuft of grass to toss at him.

He blew one of the blades away. "So you trust me even on the days you wish to do bodily harm to me?" He loved her smile; he watched her for a few moments as she laughed at his question, and then he sighed as she

# Beauty and the Beast

## Jenni James

StoneHouse Ink 2012
StoneHouse Ink
Boise ID 83713
http://www.stonehouseink.net

First eBook Edition: 2012
First Paperback Edition: 2012

ISBN: 978-1-938426-49-0

Cover design by Phatpuppy Art
Layout design by Ross Burck

Published in the United States of America

between the two of them.

Cecelia rested her head upon her right hand and sighed, with the other hand she pulled the shimmering necklace from where it rested under her bodice and examined the way it sparkled and shined in the moonlight. Butterflies fluttered within at the thought of meeting him again on the morrow. What would he say to her? What would she wear? All at once a thousand different questions seemed to invade her mind.

Whether he thought her brash or not did not matter. She needed this, she needed hope and courage and something magical to cling to.

A giggle of mirth bubbled out of her throat before she clamped her mouth shut and closed the curtains. Tonight was the night that dreams were made of. Tonight was when she could allow all of her thoughts to run wild and explore every hidden avenue of a new delightful relationship—a change. What would they do? What would happen from here?

She did not know, she did not care either. The most important thing at the moment was

# Chapter Seventeen

CECELIA RAN ALL the way to her house chastising herself for her silliness and immaturity. How could she have just blurted that without waiting to see his reaction? What girl went around proclaiming her love to the male species anyhow? Wasn't that their responsibility? What must he think of such brash and forward behavior? Her blush deepened at the thought.

Once in her room, she threw her cloak upon the bench and walked to the window overlooking the beautiful forest below her. There was something different in the air. As if her words created some sort of change that she was with him forever.

Long after she had gone to sleep, Miss Cecelia Hammerstein-Smythe had a very contented smile upon her lips. The world was hers, if she would but open her eyes and see the great possibilities awaiting her.

PRINCE ALEXANDER DUSTED himself off and began the long walk home. He was still a bit stunned—complete and utter shock, actually. She had done it. The gel had fallen in love with him. And what had he done to receive such a blessing? Nothing. Nothing of significance. Yet, his most unattainable dreams became reality.

Dear, dear Cecelia! She was indeed the most incredible woman he had ever known.

And what a lesson to him in that moment! The final blow of all his worthlessness and great follies of his youth. Half a year ago, he was nothing but young and selfish—now, she has had made a man of him.

Was it truly that easy to create love? To create great trust?

How many people had he mocked because

of their unfortunate looks? How many of
his own subjects had he shamed with his
insensitive and harsh behavior? And yet, what
he believed would never happen because of his
own appearance, did.

Oh, what he would give to swing her
up in his arms this very second and tell her
everything he'd wish to say from the very
beginning. He'd been such an idiot, such a
complete and utter fool all of his life. And no
one save that witch could have proven to him
what a monster he'd become. He owed the old
woman everything. His life, his love, his great
change of heart—she was indeed a saint in his
eyes. Without her, he would have never been
humbled enough to know the great love of his
life. To experience this happiness bursting all
around him.

Once within the castle grounds, he
rushed to her tombstone. After Alexander
had sufficiently seen the wisdom of the
old woman, he'd ordered that her body be
removed and brought to receive a proper burial
within the royal grounds. He placed her right
next to the great kings where she belonged.
His eyes travelled over the chiseled words he

had placed upon the tombstone.

> *Here lies a wise woman of great worth.*
> *A woman whose deeds changed a nation.*
> *A woman whose life shall be heralded*
> *here out*
> *And celebrated for centuries to come.*
> *Thank you for all you have done for your*
> *kingdom.*
> *You are blessed. You are loved. You are*
> *honored.*

Kneeling before the large stone, he thanked her. "I owe you my whole life, may I please come to you and offer my deepest gratitude for all you have taught me and all that I am? Thank you, my dear lady, thank you." His hands clasped and he rocked slightly forward as he spoke. "She did it. You are probably more amazed than I, but she did it. That sweet, perfect girl broke the spell. I cannot believe it has been less than a year and already I am free. Do I deserve to be free? Have I become all you had wished for me to learn then?"

Turning around he rested his back against

the chiseled marble. "I wish you could meet Cecelia. I think you would approve and I know she would have loved you. Anyone who could have put me in my place would have no doubt been highly honored by her." He smiled.

"Do you know what I will do to thank you? I've been thinking about it lately, and I believe I will construct a large rose garden in your honor. A beautiful winding pathed escape, with the finest roses in the world to adorn its walls and beautiful sculptures and fountains to complement the serene nature. I think it's perfect to represent not only the relationship between me and Cecelia, but also to respect a wise woman who knew greater than I did the importance of humility. Though, the thorns of the rose are prickly and hard to bear—as all great trials are—the delicate petals are velvety smooth and glorious unlike any description, and worth all the thorns it took to create them.

"Thank you for allowing me to see the beauty in the world. It was worth every single prick of the thorns that came my way."

By the time he'd approached the castle,

Alexander had forgotten all about Lord
Bellemount and the servants' search for him
earlier. It wasn't until he was met at the
door by an anxious footman that he realized
anything was amiss.

"What is it, Tom?" he asked the boy, about
sixteen or seventeen.

"It's Lord Bellemount, your highness. We
captured him!"

Excitement and anger simultaneously
coursed through the prince, as he recalled the
day's accusations. "You did? Where did you
find him?"

"Out in the monument garden hiding
behind a statue near the north wall."

"Take me to him immediately."

"Yes, your highness. Dalton thought to
have him placed in the fruit cellar until you
returned."

He followed the servant as they wound
through the halls, into the kitchen and around
several other excited staff members, down the
stairs and into the cellar.

Alexander ducked his head as he entered
the carved doorway into the cold, dimly lit
stone-walled room. His cousin was gagged

and strapped to a chair with two of the brawny stable boys on either side of him. "Well, well, Frederick, I see we can add trespassing to your list of crimes." To the makeshift guards he said, "It is fine, boys. I can handle it from here. Please wait outside the door so I can talk to him privately."

"Your highness," they chorused and nodding a quick bow left Alexander alone with his cousin.

Lord Bellemount's eyes were huge as the prince walked over and removed the gag. Then just as Frederick was about to speak, Alexander swung back and slammed his fist into his cousin's jaw.

Frederick howled and rubbed his reddening jowl on his shoulder.

"If you so much as look at Miss Hammerstein-Smythe again, I will do much worse." Alexander leaned over the chair and grabbed his collar. "Do I make myself perfectly clear?"

His cousin nodded, the sting of the punch watering his eyes.

"My father taught me that violence was never the answer; however, if you harm her in any way—or even offend her nose with your smell in her very vicinity—I will resort to extreme violence to deal with you. I. Have. Had. Enough."

"Wait!" he whined. "You know it was just a lark, something for a laugh. You know I would never—"

"A lark! A laugh?" The prince yanked on his shirt. "You call falsely accusing me of degrading the woman I love, to her face, a lark?"

"I had no idea!"

"You had every single idea of sabotaging our relationship!" He shoved his cousin away and took a couple of agitated steps around the room and then turned. "What I want to understand is why. Why would you do this to me and to her? Why, Frederick? Why risk your own possibility to become prince, for this? Are you out of your mind?!"

"Prince?! You were not going to give me the throne if you married her!"

The room went silent.

Water dripped from somewhere very near, but the barrels of fruit and shelves of cheeses warped the sound enough to not be able to locate it.

Alexander sighed. "So this is why you followed me the other night?" He put his hand on his waist, flipping his coat aside. "This is why you sought to destroy the first good thing I have ever had in my life. Because you were jealous?"

"Do you blame me?"

"Yes, you fool! Until tonight, I would have had no choice anyhow. The throne would have been yours—relationship with Miss Hammerstein-Smythe or not, I could have never ruled as a wolf!"

"I do not understand your meaning. I have watched you change into a wolf, but what has that got to do with anything? Other than your subjects thinking you were peculiar."

"About six months ago, I came across an old ugly woman, whose stench was among the most pungent I have ever beheld. And like all of the other times in my horrid existence up until then, I laughed at her and belittled her. There was no one else on the path except her and me, but I felt it was my right as prince to tell her to remove her hideous personage off the castle property.

Frederick laughed. "Sounds like something you would say."

"Something I would have said. Not now, not ever again, hopefully." He ran one hand through his hair. "Unbeknownst to me, the old woman would change my life completely. She was a witch, and in her grave anger, she transformed me into a beast.

"She told me I had one year, where every night I would turn into a wolf, but the stipulation to remove the curse was I had to find a girl to fall in love with me as the wolf, not as the prince. If I could not achieve that impossible fate, then I would forever become a beast.

"I had given up. I knew what a monster I was personally, and did not believe any woman would fall in love with me as a hideous animal, so was ready to abdicate the throne over to you. Then once my year was up, I could transform fully into a wolf and go into hiding, while you ran the affairs of the country. However, all that changed tonight when, as Cecelia was leaving, she announced she was in love with me—the wolf me. I immediately transformed into the prince she despises—my appreciations to you—but she'd already left by the time I did."

"Just a moment, so Miss Hammerstein-Smythe has no idea the wolf she loves is gone? And will never return? And she has no idea that wolf was you?"

"No. None at all."

Frederick rubbed his lips together for a moment before clarifying, "And she does not like the prince, correct?"

Alexander glared. "I would not bring that point up often, if I were you."

Lord Bellemount smirked. "It would seem you find yourself in quite a pickle, cuz. What will you do about it?"

Alexander did not trust the look upon his face, part sneering, part vengeful. "The only thing I'm going to do currently," he leaned over placing a hand on either side of Frederick's shoulders, "is guarantee you do not leave this room until I can decide what country to ship you to."

"What?" Lord Bellemount whimpered, "You can't do that. Not now, not—"

The prince placed the gag back over his mouth. "I have no reliance in you, and I never

will again." He whispered in his ear. "You,
my nearest relation, will not be recognized
by me and mine anymore. You as of this
moment are stripped of your title and you are
very fortunate I do not have you hanged for
treason." He pulled up and looked him in the
eye. "Do you understand, Frederick? It is
over; you will not bother myself or the woman
I hope to make my wife again."

With that said he called the guards in
and placed them completely in charge of
his brainless cousin. "I will deal with you
tomorrow, Frederick. Goodnight. May you
enjoy your cool slumber."

Alexander brushed thoughts of his cousin
aside and took the stairs two at a time as he
began to plot his plan of attack. He had one
very lovely young woman's heart to claim and
declare it to be his forever.

The prince smiled. It would be quite the
challenge, knowing Cecelia's temperament and
gumption, but it would definitely be worth it.

# Chapter Eighteen

FREDERICK WORKED ON his bands all night long. After he had complained about the bright candles while trying to sleep, the guards were quick to put them out, leaving the cellar black enough to untie himself in silence without anyone being the wiser. It took about three and a half hours of constant tugging and pulling, but he was finally able to get one hand free. Then it was a matter of minutes before the second one, and then the legs. By the time he had tiptoed past the guards and made his way out the servants' entrance of the castle it was nearing four o'clock.

He rushed out of the grounds before the

servants began to wake. Already the faint
stirring of smoke could be seen rising from a
few of the chimneys. Figuring he had a couple
hours to get home and packed before his own
family woke up.

Once there, he raided the family reservoirs
of money. He loaded one small purse full to
brimming of their hidden stash of fortune, as
well as packing in a separate bag a few of his
favorite odds and ends; books, trinkets and the
like. Rushing to the kitchen, he managed to
pilfer some cheese and a loaf of bread Cook
had just brought out of the oven, while her
back was turned. Then as an afterthought he
grabbed the kitchen knife as well. Saddling
his horse, he placed everything into the
larger-sized traveling pouches that sat on
its haunches. And then he was gone, racing
toward a house that looked very similar to
Miss Hammerstein-Smythe's home.

He had one more visit to make before he
left this country forever.

Indeed, it served his cousin right for
treating him as he did. If one was to be
punished as a criminal, one should at least
have the opportunity to act the villain first.

Frederick smiled.

The glorious sun was high enough to begin streaming over the hilltops, washing everything beneath it in a glow of serenity. The birds chirped happily above as he rode and the smells of summer were in full bloom all around him. Truly, there could not be a more enchanted day if he'd planned it, an absolutely perfect day for destroying one lovely gel.

CECELIA AWOKE TO a strange splattering sound upon her window. It took a few more moments before she comprehended someone was pelting small stones upon the glass. With an eerie feeling, she slipped on her robe and opened the curtains. Peering down into the small courtyard below she was surprised to see Lord Bellemount awake and dressed, especially at this hour!

"Miss Hammerstein-Smythe, I need to speak to you immediately," he hissed. "Could you come down and meet me in the rose garden? It's a matter of most urgent importance."

Cecelia's heart tightened and sank. Something was not right. Her arms began to quiver and feel heavy. Undeniably, something was not correct in this invitation at all, as if her soul were pleading with her to stay where she was. She knew this feeling—dread. And could not shake it enough to come down and meet him, no matter how important the message. "I fear I cannot. My maid will wake."

An unexpected flash of anger flew across his features. "No. You must come down this very moment. It is of great import that I deliver this message now."

The feeling of trepidation grew stronger. Her heart began to race. He was not in a healthy state of mind. No manner of inducements he urged would allow her to risk the safety of her home to face him below. "Leave a message at the door, Sanford will deliver it to me, and await my reply."

Frederick was livid. He had hoped to lure her into the rose garden where he had placed the great kitchen knife under a bush, but the dim-witted girl would not come to him.

Just as she was about to close the windows

he frantically searched his mind and whispered in great urgency, "It is about Prince Alexander. He has killed the wolf!"

Cecelia's heart jolted to a halt as she flung the windows open wider. "What did you say?"

"I know about the beast you have fallen in love with. Alexander was wild with jealousy when the wolf told him about you and had him slaughtered this very morning." When he saw her face he added, "Oh, it was torture to hear his howls of anguish. They were so loud and so tortured, I've never experienced such sounds of pain from a beast before."

"No!" Huge gulps of air did not help her lungs prepare for the onslaught of utter hopelessness and destruction she felt. Her hand flew to her mouth and travelled on its own accord all over her face, her brow, her chin, her neck, trying to make sense of the horror she was hearing.

"He urged me, on his last dying breath, to send a message to you. He loves you! He told me so himself!"

She could not speak, she could not function.

"Please, come down here. I must tell you

everything."

"Yes, yes," she whispered in numbed shock. "I'll be there in a trice."

She closed the window, then the thick curtains, allowing her room to be swallowed up in darkness. As if in a trance she threw a dress at random over her nightgown, slipped her feet into some sturdy boots, fetched her woolen cape and snuggled it tightly around her and then promptly fell upon the bed.

Her life was over. There was nothing left for her now.

Deep aching sadness enveloped her and a dull buzzing began in her ears, cocooning her from the world and all of its horrors below. She laid there for several minutes, never giving another thought to the anxious Lord waiting for her.

It was after some time, once she began to imagine the wolf in agony, his howls filling the sky—his last words of her—that the bitter tears began. She was done. She was broken. There was nothing anyone could do to save her from this grief now.

It was over.

THE PRINCE HAD meant to go immediately
to Cecelia and proclaim all, but when he was
informed of the escaped convict, he spent
the day scouring and searching for him.
Every servant was on hand to look for Lord
Bellemount—and several hired villagers as
well.

At Bellemount Manor it was discovered
he had been there and taken off with most of
the family fortune and treasures. Alexander
traced his trail as far as the village, and then to
the docking yard. He felt a sigh of relief when
many people had spotted him boarding a ship
that was just about to set sail.

"Stop that ship!" he shouted loud enough
to be heard over the noisy dock. "By order of
the prince, I command you to halt that vessel
and allow me onboard. You are harboring a
prisoner of mine."

It took several minutes for the crew to
lower the anchor and situate the plank again.
Once on the ship, Alexander wasted no time
issuing orders for every available hand to

search for his wayward cousin. His own men
shouting and searching along with the crew as
he went below, the smell of the sea was strong
and seemed to permeate the polished wood as
he walked along a narrow hallway and began
to search several rooms.

"Yer Majesty! Yer Majesty!" hissed one
of the shipmen beckoning to him as he walked
out of yet another room bereft of his cousin, "I
believe the man yer lookin' fer is hiding in that
there cupboard." He pointed to a small door at
the end of the hallway. "I saw him run in there
with me own two eyes after the ship began
dockin' again."

"Thank you." He nodded to the man and
rushed to the door, pounding sharply before
swinging it wide open. Frederick was indeed
inside, barely squeezed amongst the rags,
brushes, buckets and lye soap stored around
him. Without wasting another moment, he
yanked on his cousin's collar and hauled him
out of the cupboard into the hallway with one
swing of his arm.

"And where do you think you are going?"

"How did you find me?" Frederick's
voice shook as his hand clutched the handle

of the knife behind his back. He may be frightened out of his wits but he was definitely not afraid to do something about it.

"I have my ways," answered the prince as he began to drag him back toward the stairs.

As soon as Alexander had given him a clear opening, Frederick took his opportunity and lunged the hidden knife into the prince's side.

Alexander went stiff from the shock. Then like an accordion he began to sway and stagger, folding into himself as one shoulder collided with the wall.

Lord Bellemount felt his throat tighten painfully as Alexander's hand fisted around his collar, cutting off his air supply. The prince slowly slid down the wall taking his cousin with him. Frederick frantically clawed at the fabric and fingers trying to loosen and regain any fraction of air he could. Alexander's fist was iron and could not be pried apart and the fabric was too tight to catch hold of.

Shouting could be heard off at a distance and Frederick could make out the short, painful gasps of the prince. As they slipped the last couple of feet, his head thunked against the floor and the world around him began to grow blurry. His last thought before disappearing into oblivion was that at least the prince would die with him.

Alexander's side was on fire, the sticky wet ooze of blood seeped out of the wound making the floor too slippery to stand upon, or to regain proper footing. When he fell a moment ago, the knife lodged itself deeper into his side. He knew he had to remove the blade before it did any more damage, but his body was in such shock he could not force his fingers to release Frederick; they refused to open. His other arm was twisted painfully beneath him. Desperately he tried to twist himself to remove the weight of his body off the trapped arm. He winced at the sharp pain that shot through his frame as he irritated the wound more.

All at once the hallway began to darken as distressed faces peered down at him, he was surprised to see their mouths were moving as if they were shouting, but he could not hear a word they spoke.

Then everything went black.

# Chapter Nineteen

CECELIA WAS A complete wreck.
After several long bouts of weeping, she
remembered the prince telling her that Lord
Bellemount was not to be trusted. She also
recollected the great feeling of unease and
dread that had come over her when he insisted
on speaking in the garden.

In a desperate need to prove to herself the
wolf was surely gone, she wiped her swollen
eyes and ran to the garden, collecting a single
red rose, and carried it directly to the brook.

When she returned later, it seemed to
radiate upon the stone, giving her a small
measure of hope to cling to. She did not touch

it, but curled up alongside the little stream and waited. The melody of the meandering water did much to calm her soul, but the absence of the beast weighed heavily in her heart.

She missed him more than she'd ever missed anyone.

He never came.

She knew then he was most certainly gone forever.

Miss Hammerstein-Smythe mourned her love against the soft dewy moss until morning broke through the fragile leaves and reminded her she needed to be home. Leaving the rose, she slowly climbed the little hill and began the long walk back to the house.

Later that morning her mother entered her room, took one look at her daughter, and seemed to know that now was not the time for questions. She shut the door quietly behind her as she thankfully left Cecelia in peace.

By the time the prince had made it home the following evening, he was exhausted. The ship's surgeon had done a marvelous job stitching and caring for the deep cut.

Thankfully Frederick had missed any vital
organs. He stayed onboard the docked ship
the first night, in the captain's cabin. Against
the wishes of the surgeon and his servants,
he demanded to return home when he had
awakened.

As he was waiting for the royal carriage
to be brought from the palace—since riding
home was out of the question—he was able
to see his cousin's body one last time before
the crew bundled him up and tossed him
overboard, where all traitors, thieves and
tyrants go. He saw that his items were packed
up and sent back with the castle guards to
be taken to his family later. The shipmen
said Frederick had died sometime during the
night. The moment Alexander had become
unconscious; his fingers had loosened their
grip, allowing Frederick to breath. However,
it was too late. After a few hours of ragged
breathing, he passed away.

The prince thankfully walked into his
quarters at the castle, his sides bandaged under
his shirt. It was only around seven o'clock
at night, but the weariness of his stress and
healing, as well as the months of interrupted

sleep as a wolf, seemed to all meld into one.
He could finally, for the very first night,
slumber in peace. After helping himself to
supper, he dressed in his nightclothes and
padded over to his bed, crashing upon its
billowy softness until nearly ten the next
morning.

When the prince awoke, his eyes rested
upon the wearied collection of roses he had
near his bed and he cursed his own folly
at forgetting the sweet Miss Hammerstein-
Smythe. In the confusion caused by his
cousin, and the relief the villain could
no longer harm anyone again, he'd quite
forgotten all about the gel. Or the fact she had
proclaimed her love to him and had been most
likely anxiously waiting the wolf to make an
appearance last night.

How could he have been so slow? Where
was his brain?

Despite the fretting of his staff, he
anxiously ate, shaved and dressed, eager to be
out the door and make up for the time already
wasted by his despicable cousin. Before he

called to have his coach brought round to the front of the castle, he slipped a beautiful diamond-and-emerald ring into the front inside pocket of his jacket. He would bedeck her in many more jewels than this ring once they were wed, but for the time being it was perfect.

The ring had belonged to his great-grandmother and had cost his grandfather a king's ransom to create it for her. She too was a villager who had caught the prince's heart. At the time when the intricate ring had been made, there had been nothing as striking in the entire kingdom. She wore it with great pride, though to the day she died she still proclaimed he could have fashioned a ring of mere string and she would have been happy.

Their love was something Alexander never believed truly existed until now. Until his own charming Cecelia opened his eyes to the possibility of a perfect union.

Climbing into the carriage, the coachman took off with a flash, arriving in all eagerness at Miss Hammerstein-Smythe's home just before noon.

She would not see him.

Nothing her mother, the servants, or any letter he sent up to her room by way of a messenger would be responded to.

He must speak with her! He must unravel what was wrong so that he could have some way of fixing the tangled web they found themselves in. And yet, he could not believe she had even read a single one of his letters he had sent to her while he cooled his heels in the best parlor.

Prince Alexander was correct; Cecelia had burnt each missive she received from the servants into the fireplace of her room, before reading them. She would not go down; she would not speak to him ever again. She could not forgive, nor would she allow herself to pardon the man who had ruined every chance of happiness she had.

How dare he attempt to show up at her door now.

How dare he have the gumption to believe she would receive him.

Her wolf was gone, and he had no one but himself to blame. And yet, she should welcome him into her arms? Never. Never again would she so much as speak to the horrid man!

An hour or so later brought the same splattering sound against her window as the day before had. She opened it to find this time the prince himself below. "Go away!" she called down before shutting the window again.

"Cecelia!" he shouted, but the glass had been closed up and she pretended not to hear him. He stood below her room shouting up at the window for a good twenty minutes, demanding to speak to her, asking what was wrong, and drawing way too many eyes and ears in their direction for comfort.

She knew the neighbors would be having a heyday with this and the thought is what actually prompted her to open the window again. "Prince Alexander, be gone with you. I cannot stand to hear your hollering another moment. I do not wish to speak to you. I despise you and I never, ever want to see you again!"

Miss Hammerstein-Smythe watched in amazement as he shrugged his shoulders, smiled at something to the left of him, and said, "As you wish," before sauntering off.

He left? She could not approve of how

he could have gone so easily. Stepping away from the sill, she walked around her room for a few minutes. What had he wanted to say to her? Did he have a reason for killing the beast she was not aware of? Did he have more lies to spew or more mocking to commence on her behalf? She scowled and turned on her heel and then screamed at the sight of Prince Alexander leaning into her room.

"What are you doing here, sir?" she gasped exceedingly astonished. "How are you up here?"

Alexander grinned, ignoring the pain in his side. "It's a ladder. Your stable boy lent it to me. And I am here because you will not listen to me or talk to me in any other way, and I must speak with you."

Concluding she would never hear the end of it if she did not allow him to declare what he must, she said, "You have exactly a minute to say all you have to say, before I push you from the window myself." She walked up to him. "And do not for one moment believe I am not livid enough to do so!"

He saw the deep-rooted pain in her red-rimmed eyes, the hollowed circles under them and deepening in her sunken cheeks. She was literally dying inside. "Don't be sad, Cecelia, please. I have come to share a secret with you, one you may not understand or accept, but it is the truth."

Her eyes closed, not caring one wit about anything he revealed. "What is that?"

"I am the beast."

Cecelia's eyes flew open and connected with his. "Liar. You killed him!"

"What?" Never in his wildest imaginings did he expect those words to come out of her mouth.

"You heard of my love for him and murdered the only creature who has ever made me truly happy." She brought her face right up to his. "I hate you. I despise you. I loathe you!"

"No." He shook his head. "No, Cecelia, my dear, whatever account you have heard, it is false. The wolf is not dead—indeed he has changed—he is forever a man now, the enchantment is broken, but he is not dead. I promise you, it is me. It has always been me. I was tricked by an old woman and put under a spell—"

"I do not want to hear another word!" Her face contorted with pain more stark than any he had ever seen before.

"Cecelia, please…"

"Stop calling me that! Only he calls me Cecelia."

"I know," he paused and answered quietly. "It is why I do."

"Arrgh!" She pushed against him, but he held fast to the window, his side stinging from the exertion. "Go, leave me alone."

"Cecelia…" he whispered, one arm sliding around her shoulders. "Cecelia, it is me. I promise you, it is I, your Apollo."

She cried then. She did not believe one word he spoke, but she sobbed into his shoulder and closed her arms around him and clung as though her soul depended on it.

He mumbled a hundred words of endearment into her hair and she never made out one. Only the sound of his breathing and faint heartbeat found their way to her ears. She finally pushed away and would not allow her soul to hope and believe in a man she could not trust—a man who she had only ever known to be cruel until very recently.

What a twisted world she lived in. Nothing made sense. But she could not, simply could not accept he was her Apollo. It was too convenient. It was too confusing.

If he was, why would he not tell her before? Why leave her to die alone the last two evenings at the brook?

No, if he were indeed her wolf he would have known of the little stream and that she would have been waiting for him. He would have come to her. "Where were you?" She sniffled and rubbed her eyes. "If you are indeed Apollo, then where were you?" She refused to tell him of the meeting spot to see if he would tell her what she longed to hear.

His eyes searched hers, pleading to be understood and not wanting to alarm her. "I was detained."

There was something more there, something he was not saying. "I do not believe you."

"I'm sorry. I am so sorry to have left you alone like I did—when you clearly needed me most."

She shook her head; she was so very tired of the diversions and amusements of the royalty. She was not a game to be played. She would not be made sport of again. "Please leave, I cannot see you. I cannot look upon you without my heart breaking. You have crushed me beyond recognition. I ask that you please leave and never come back."

Alexander gasped. Her words sliced him more than any had before. He had nothing to do, but what she asked. He simply could not be the means of harming her more. She needed Apollo, and in her eyes he would never be the beast of her heart.

He took one long look at the only girl he had ever cherished, and whispered, "I love you," before slowly making his way down the steps and onto the garden below. Within minutes, he was heading back to his castle to mourn the loss, a tragedy so great he felt as though his body were splitting in two. Vowing to never stray from the palace again, Alexander slammed his bedroom door closed and collapsed upon the stone floor, his wound burning.

It was all in vain. It was all too late.

He had learned to love, finally—but it was too late.

Alexander felt as though he were dying, and the only thing that could save him was the one woman who could not see past the monster he once was to know of the great love within his heart.

## Chapter Twenty

AFTER THE PRINCE left, Cecelia walked down to the brook. She found so much solace there, as if Apollo's memory was living on. For a solid week she came back often. It was the only relief she felt—at her magical brook. However, it wasn't until the seventh day that her world changed and the first glimmer of happiness began to peek through the darkened clouds.

The rose was still there, though much more withered. She had placed a rock upon it a few days earlier to guarantee the flower would not blow away as it continued to dry. Cecelia trailed her fingers over the wrinkled petals. It was almost the color of crimson, much darker than the bright red when she had picked it. The hue reminded her most of the necklace he had given her. Subconsciously she pulled the heart out of her bodice, and before she knew what she was doing, held it up to the sunshine.

If she had thought it beautiful in the moonlight, it was simply splendid in the daytime. She spun it slowly around and watched the way the sunbeams danced and sparkled and bounced their way off of it. It most definitely was one of the most remarkable gifts she had ever been given.

It was as she was examining the heart, and following the path of the gold rose as it wrapped itself around it, that she noticed a small hinge under one of the tiny golden leaves. Curious, she brought the pendant closer and examined it thoroughly.

There seemed to be a small clasp hidden within another leaf. As she pressed down upon it, the rose released and the heart opened up. Cecelia gasped as a tiny scrolled piece of paper fell out of the necklace and onto her lap. With shaky hands, she opened the note and read the following—

> *"If thou could but see thy crown! The*
> *land would forge ever onward, pressing*
> *gloriously within sight. For thee, my*
> *precious moonbeam, will yet prevail the*
> *fight."*
>
> *May you always remember I have seen*
> *the crown upon your head. Never doubt*
> *your worth, my dear, for you are greater*
> *than you think you are. And soon you will*
> *be flying.*
>
> *—Alexander*

At first her heart was so full of Apollo and
the words he spoke unto her, and his amazing
conviction that she truly was more incredible
than she believed, she could not see or think
of anything else. However, once she had
shed a few tears and reread the note over and
over again enough times to allow her brain to
process the loss she believed herself to have
had, she did notice one small confusion with
the letter. There was a word there that should
not have been, and yet it was written as plain
as day:

*—Alexander*

The prince had written the missive? Was he truly Apollo? Could it be? Her heart speed began to pick up as her mind raced through the last conversation they had had together. It was difficult to remember most of it, since she had deliberately tried to push it from her mind, considering it all to be false.

But what if indeed he were the wolf?

What if it was Prince Alexander all along?! She sat up more fully, her foot tapping against the dirt. If he were the prince, then that would explain why Alexander knew everything about her so quickly. It would explain why he did not flinch when others thought they were engaged. He was trying to help in the only way he knew how. And it would also explain why she felt so secure around the prince, because it was the same being; he was the same soul!

Her mind zinged and pinged through several displaced and muddled conversations with the beast as well, especially upon his last one that said there were many things he couldn't tell her. How he wasn't always a wolf, how he was under an enchantment.

In agitation, Cecelia stood and began to pace.

It made absolutely no sense.

It made perfect sense.

No, no. It couldn't be. He couldn't possibly have been her wolf all along.

And if he was, then what changed? Why was he no longer a beast? What had broken the spell? And why would Lord Bellemount lie to her?

"Ugh." She grunted a very unladylike grunt and kicked a small stone into the stream. Dare she believe any of this for a mere moment? Dare she allow her heart the freedom to hope again?

Alexander had told her over and over she could trust the wolf; the beast also believed the prince to be extremely trustworthy. If they were the same person, would it not make more sense?

A small sob escaped, and she quickly suppressed it with her hand. It couldn't be. He couldn't still be hers. Not now, not after all this time when she believed he was gone.

She folded her arms and looked up at the sky, trying to find some sort of divine guidance, something that could steer her soul into knowing what to do and who to believe.

After a minute or so of silence, she realized what it was she must do to prove to herself once and for all if he was indeed her dear Apollo. Scurrying home, she bypassed the gate and went straight to her mother's rose garden. Finding a large pink rose, full of hope and blossoming joy, she picked it and made her way to the castle.

Once there she placed the rose upon the step of the large front door.

If he were indeed Apollo, Alexander would know it as a sign to meet her at the brook that evening. If he were not, then it would just remain an insignificant rose placed upon the steps of the castle, and no one would ever understand its meaning.

As she was leaving, she nearly bumped into one of the servants, a boy coming up to the palace.

"Are you here to see his Highness?" asked the boy.

"No." She pointed to the flower. "I have

only come to deliver a rose for him. Will you see that he finds it?"

"Yes, ma'am." The boy bowed and hurried on his way.

Cecelia smiled and breathed a sigh of relief knowing that at least he would have the opportunity to see the rose before someone removed it. She quickly left the castle grounds and made her way back home. Excitement fissured through her as she allowed a small fraction of hope to take place of the horrid melancholy she'd felt lately.

Oh, please let it be him!

Please let her mind be correct, just this once.

Her mother's incessant chatter did nothing to still the ever-blossoming excitement growing within her. It was all Cecelia could do to remain calm and eat dinner and pretend as if her world was not all of the sudden perhaps on the brink of becoming completely altered yet again.

She chose a stunning gown of blue silk and brushed out the curls that she had allow to fall down her back lately—not caring if her hair were up or down. This evening, however, she pinned her hair up herself, not hoping to alarm her maid, and was amazed at the beautiful style she was able to create. She pinched some color into her cheeks and smiled at the girl before her in the looking glass. It had been too long since her eyes sparkled back at her in such a way.

As soon as the sun went down, Cecelia hurried to the stream with a lightness in her step, eager to get there before he did. Removing the dead rose, she sat down upon the stone and arranged her gown prettily in an arch around her feet, and adjusted her necklace to shine in the moonlight.

And then she waited.

## Chapter Twenty-One

PRINCE ALEXANDER CAME over the hill, with the rose in hand, just moments after she had settled herself. He too could not remain an instant longer, and was hoping to be there and await her arrival, but as he saw, she was as eager as he.

He paused and watched her for a minute or two, taking in the superb sight before him. Cecelia had not noticed his arrival as of yet, and therefore it allowed a moment for him to catch his breath and wonder at the great gift he had been granted. Had she forgiven him? Did she finally believe he was the beast? Was she willing to put the past aside and begin again?

Whatever the outcome of tonight, it was important to note she indeed was willing to speak to him—nay, she beckoned him with the flower. No matter what else happened, this was enough. This was a start and a chance to prove again he had changed before her eyes.

Cecelia looked up then and a smile wreathed her countenance as she caught sight of him. She was standing and walking toward Alexander before he'd even made it a step in her direction. "You came," she said simply as she approached. And then after searching his features, her hand coming up to rest upon his jaw she said, "Is it, in fact, you? Are you truly my dear Apollo?"

"I am, I always have been."

"Oh, Alexander, I am so sorry. Can you ever forgive me?"

"For what? What did you do that could—?"

"Forgive me for not doing this when I had the opportunity." She then reached up on tiptoe and pulled his jaw down to her own and kissed him in a soft, tender kiss.

Alexander wrapped her up in his arms, pulling her feet right off the ground. His heart thumped wildly in his ears until he could think of nothing but her mouth on his. When he set her back down and pulled slightly away, his arms still around her, he said, "I'm afraid, my dear, I will never let you go now that you've decided to like me again."

Cecelia laughed and corrected him. "My prince, I love you. There is no liking about this relationship that I can tell, only perfect unconditional love."

"Yes," he said, "yes, this is definitely what unconditional love means." His voice cracked as he continued, "Cecelia, how did you ever fall in love with a hideous beast?"

Her gaze searched his as she shook her head a bit, trying to convey something he would never understand. "Because it was you. I would have loved you, this—the true you"—she rubbed her palm over his heart—"in any form you came to me in. I know this soul, and it is good and wise and beautiful. Even when I did not recognize you as the prince, I couldn't stay away." Her hand wound up playing with the hairs at the back of his neck. "And because you cared for me when no one else did. You worried and loved me like no being ever has before. Because you are the most dearest creature that has ever lived." She brazenly kissed him again and said, "Alexander, I do not understand what has happened to you, or why, but my heart breaks at the pain you must have faced. And yet, it swells at the joy that brought you to me, for without you, I would be nothing. You are my life, my dreams, my joy."

"No." His eyes traced her features lovingly. "You are the angel here. You, who should have never had to endure my company again—you who should never have to forgive a monster like I was to you, you are here before me and saying that you are in love. Cecelia, this cannot be. I do not deserve a love as perfect as this. I do not deserve anything. I had resigned myself to my fate. I believed I was worth nothing more than the animal form I became every night. And yet, you—you saw past that façade to a person I did not even know existed. You, my dear, are my life, my dreams, my joy. Without you I have nothing. I am nothing."

She threw back her head and giggled, she couldn't help herself, everything was so very serious so quickly. "I believe we are both everything to the other, yes?"

He smiled. "Yes."

"Good." She moved out of his arms and pulled his hand walking him over to the brook. After he sat down, she joined him and snuggled into his chest, her skirts billowing behind her.

"This is highly improper." His baritone sent shivers down her spine.

"Mm-hm. I know." She grinned into his waistcoat. "But it feels so wonderful, does it not?"

His arms tightened their hold. "Most definitely."

She sighed as she listened to the thud, thud, thud of his heart, marveling that he was indeed very much alive.

"Cecelia."

"Yes?" she mumbled.

"Will you marry me?"

She wrapped her arms around his waist and giggled. "I don't know, should I?"

"Yes, most definitely. If not, it would look very odd when I hauled you up to my castle and held you captive."

"Alexander!" she playfully gasped.

"What?" He pulled back to see her expression. "You don't think I have it in me to hold you captive, my dear?"

"I don't know. As I recall it was me who managed to stun you with that stick." She raised an eyebrow and grinned. "Perhaps it is you who should be worried about me keeping you prisoner."

The prince laughed, his deep rumble causing her chest to glow. "I believe I will let you have this one, I wouldn't want you clubbing me to death in a surprise attack."

"Yes."

"Yes, I know you—"

"Yes, I will marry you."

He looked down into her quite sudden serious countenance.

She said, "I cannot be without you again. I do not want to lose you, I couldn't. Not now, not ever."

Alexander brushed a few stray hairs away from her brow. "Thank you." And then he smiled a very mischievous—almost wolfish—grin and said, "Of course, I think perhaps we should bring the matter up slowly with your mother this time. I do not want to have to lift her after she's swooned again."

Cecelia laughed. "Well, it's good to know some things about you will never change."

"Meaning?"

"Your uncanny lack of charm, of course!"

Alexander kissed her then, quite perfectly and thoroughly until they were both ragged from breathing.

Much later under the moonlight, he slipped the beautiful emerald ring on her finger. And even later than that, they discussed his ordeal, how it was he became a beast, and what had happened to his cousin.

"What? You were injured and you came to see me? Are you mad?"

Alexander grinned.

"Do not dare to grin down at me like that! Risking your health because of my silliness does not make me happy! I cannot believe you would put your life in peril confronting the imbecile to begin with, let alone—"

"I love you." He kissed the tip of her nose.

"Alexander, do not—"

He stopped her commentary with a kiss

to her mouth, which did not lessen the tirade she wished to wring upon his head, but did, however, tame it down a bit. And after several minutes of her clucking and cooing and concerning herself over him, Cecelia in turn told about her own dealings with Frederick and the necklace and the hidden latch she had found with the note signed by him.

After hearing of the deceit of his cousin, the prince no longer mourned his death and could very well conclude that Lord Bellemount may have continuously made their lives miserable. But it was the mention of his own signature that shocked the prince most.

"It was signed 'Alexander'? Are you sure?"

"Quite positive."

"I had no idea I had even signed the note, I must have done so out of pure habit alone."

"Whatever it was, I'm grateful you did, or I wouldn't be in your arms now enjoying the magical night with my wolfly prince."

He smiled and shook his head, snuggling her closer to him. "Thank you for seeing me, Cecelia. I know of no girl who would've cared about me as you have."

She smirked. "You know, ironically, Cecelia means 'blind.' And if anyone could fit that description, it is most definitely me!"

Alexander laughed and said, "Well, my name means 'defender,' so perhaps you can learn to trust me after all, my blind soon-to-be princess."

She rolled her eyes and cuddled back into him. "I trusted you already; I just had to open my eyes to see it."

SIX WEEKS LATER the banns were read, and three weeks after that the beautiful Miss Cecelia Hammerstein-Smythe and the most handsome Prince Alexander were wed over the altar in the palace chapel. She was splendidly dressed in white organza and imported lace, holding a bouquet of the most exquisite multi-colored roses—picked from her mother's garden, of course—and he in his dashing princely uniform of purple, cream and gold. Together they were a very striking couple.

The groom made a point to invite every single one of the villagers so they could bask in the glory of Cecelia's honor. No more gossiping and backlash toward her would be tolerated again. She was the future queen of their livelihood, and they made a point to recognize such a fact, bowing generously low, as they ought, over her hand.

An invitation was also sent to Lord Willington, but he graciously declined, of course. His bride did lament the fact she could not attend, but after buying her a new puppy that chewed his shoes, slippers, and boots to smithereens, she was happy again. And life continued on in the Willingtons' household as well as could be expected.

Mrs. Hammerstein-Smythe was said to be the happiest of all. Her joys and crows and excitements could be heard for years after the union. In fact, if the prince were not so dastardly strict with his counsel on gossiping about his wife's family—it would have been the mother-in-law who would have received the brunt of it. As it was, the villagers had to do the inner grumblings within their own homes and pretend all was well everywhere else.

Cecelia could not have honestly cared less. Her life was complete; she'd found a man to adore her just the way she was. And no matter if he were a prince or a wolf, she loved him anyway. It was not shortly afterward that the castle began to crawl with princes and princesses of its very own, which broadened and widened the great love she had for her husband even more.

As for our dear Alexander, he found that an abundant life was a reward for those who treated others kindly. And a day never went by, from that time forth, where he did not mutter thanks to the old wise woman for teaching him the true value of beauty. He did build that rose garden in her honor, and what a glory it was to behold. So stunning!

He had to, because he learned through the lesson of petals and thorns and a pretty girl, that you are only worth how good your soul truly is.

And she felt he was priceless.

***Next in the Jenni James
Faerie Tale Collection***

*Sleeping Beauty*

## Chapter One:

QUEEN ALEYNA'S EYES fluttered open
and she smiled at the shimmering sunlight
which streamed through her bedroom curtains.
Another beautifully perfect day. She stretched
and wiggled her toes under the navy blue
crushed velvet duvet and slipped out of the
golden sheets to pad across the floor to her
window.

The world beneath her castle tower was bathed in a sea of greens and yellows and glorious multicolored blossoming bushes and trees. Her village was nestled among the rolling hills and streams and winding cobblestone paths that jutted out all around the lower portion of the mountain, where her castle was happily situated, and spread to the valley below. Many homesteads and farms and fields of bounteous crops covered the great landscape as far as the eye could see.

Indeed Aleyna's kingdom was one of the most sought after and desired realms in all the world. She could not believe her good fortune in having such a prosperous and superior land. Her subjects were also known to be quite magnificent and studious in their own way as well. And to reward them for their kindness and diligence she always guaranteed they were treated above that of other monarchies and rulers around.

Her people were given several holidays each year, multiple gifts of food, household supplies, adornments and even many frivolous items would find their way into their homes from their dear queen. How she loved them.

How she loved her land, her people, her life.

It was undeniably faultless.

An enchanted kingdom to be glorified and loved by all.

Aleyna sighed in contentment as she rested her head against the smoothly-plastered stone wall and looked out the windowpane. The birds chattered and chirped and flew in delightful winging dances in the sky as they popped in and out of wistful clouds. Here was joy. Here was life at its best and she could never imagine desiring anything more.

And yet, if one could step back and but see the tragedy behind her contentment, one would know that all she witnessed below her, all she imagined above, all her hopes and dreams—were just that—dreams.

An illusion.

Queen Aleyna's life was so desperately heartrending, so tragically sorrowful, that one would need to enchant the beautiful queen and all those surrounding her and with her—all of her dear subjects—into a state of never ending bliss.

To allow her to unknowingly sleep through this horror, to allow her to heal through the pain she could not feel, to keep her from all those memories that would threaten to disarm and own her—she had to be kept in such a state. Until one who was worthy enough could come along and teach her, hold her, comfort her, release the joyful spell surrounding her contentment, and more importantly kiss her awake to the true being that was hers.

Until then, until one such worthy man came into her life and bravely fought those demons who sought to destroy her, Queen Aleyna's existence was perpetually on hold.

And she was forever trapped within a state of no progression, wrapped in a bubble of peace, and eternally asleep—as if she were a ghost—to the harsh realities awaiting her. Ignorant to all but what she knew and could remember, she would be forever known as the Sleeping Queen...

PRINCE DARIEN LAUGHED as he dodged another wayward thrust of the king's sword.

At this rate he and Michael, the King of Alemade, would be at it all night. He hooted as his friend lunged forward again. And as Darien quickly sidestepped the attack he could not help but taunt him, "Is this the greatest you've got within you? How can you hope to defend yourself, let alone a whole kingdom?"

The king grunted and swung his sword, missing the prince by a good six inches. "Perhaps if you held still long enough, I could show you how good my maneuvers are!"

Darien chuckled and took a step back, his foot slipping slightly on the wet grass of the castle lawn, before deftly lifting his sword and blocking two more wild attempts from Michael. "Admit defeat, old man, and I may let you live to see another day." It was the same thing he said to the king each week as they practiced, and true to form his friend was quick to respond in kind.

"If you weren't such a coward and could fight like a real man, I'd be able to blacken your lights for you instantly."

"Aw, yes, but we're not using fisticuffs, now are we? In fact we're—"

"And another thing! I am not an old

man." The king huffed as he haphazardly sliced his blade through the air. "I—" He stepped forward. "—am only—" Steel smacked against steel. "—five years older than you." Michael wiped his brow and cursed Darien's impeccable sword fighting skills, it was impossible to attempt to break through any of his defenses. "And the last time I checked, you were twenty-five years old."

"Yes, but twenty-seven is still much younger than you!" Darien took two steps forward arching his blade in the air and swiftly popping Michael's sword right out of his hand. It flew gracefully, allowing the handle to be caught up by the prince signifying the game was at an end.

Michael was drenched in sweat while Darien looked as though he had merely taken a leisurely stroll upon the grounds. "One of these days I am going to learn your secret," said the king as he wiped his mouth on his shirtsleeve.

"My secret?" Darien walked over to the bush where they had hung their royal coats twenty minutes earlier, placing the swords down, he collected them. "And what secret is this?" He raised a dashing brow as he handed Michael's bright green coat back to him.

The king shook the garment and waved off the servant who had run up to help, before slipping his arms into the sleeves. "Your ability to look so dashed cool and unaffected—so debonair—whilst in the midst of dueling, no less."

Darien's eyes twinkled as he put on his coat of navy and silver trimmings. "Didn't you know? Us single men must practice these things in the looking glasses at home, just during such an occasions as these, for who is to know whether a stunning female will not come by and catch us looking a spectacle." When the king grunted, he continued, "Well, you do have Cassandra, you know. And she is by far everything on this good earth that is praiseworthy indeed. But, with such a woman at your side and as your queen, be grateful you do not have to practice like I do."

Michael raised his eyes heavenward briefly as he straightened the coat over his tan colored breeches. "If I believed half the nonsense you sputtered out, I'd be a very foolish man," he said, before walking to the bush, collecting his sword, and sliding it within its sheath.

Darien laughed as he buttoned the coat. "You'd be a very foolish old man."

"You know, I'd watch your crowing if I were you." The king smirked and turned around. "Remember, boy, I know what truly does put you out of countenance—what you are most afraid of in all the world. So do not keep spouting your old jokes, for I can guarantee I can make you squirm and sweat just like the rest of us."

The prince snorted and walked over to his sword. He titled his head to the side and smugly grinned as he looked up at Michael while sliding the blade in its scabbard. "There is nothing I'm afraid of on this globe. Nothing at all—so whatever you have against me, remember it is merely a child's imaginings."

"Oh-ho! First I am too old, and now I am a child who imagines?"

"That is not what I meant, and you know it." Darien's gaze settled on his friend, they were almost brothers—had been raised like brothers—and there was no one he trusted more. The redheaded king was handsome, extremely so and had a beautiful blonde queen at his side to prove it. They'd begun to have a score of adorable little redheads and blondes themselves, and with the birth of the last one—a little girl all fiery curls and giggles— Darien founding himself longing to settle down as well. If only he could find a woman half as agreeable as Cassandra, he might just do it too.

But this sort of thinking would get him nowhere. He cleared his throat and explained, "I meant that whatever you believe me to be afraid of, was most likely something you conjured up back when we were boys. So if in reality, I am afraid of it—which I highly doubt—then it was something that I've long past put behind me."

The king smiled and patted him on the back. "I'm not discussing spiders or girls here. I'm talking about something much more terrifying in your eyes. In fact, I know you would change color at this moment if I were to speak of it, so lifeless and cold would you become."

Darien pulled away laughing and began to head back toward the castle. "There is nothing you could say that would frighten me. Nothing." He glanced back and waited for his friend to catch up to him. "Though, I am very curious what you believe you have got against me. Indeed this may be the most intriguing thing I've come upon all morning."

"Should I tell you then?" asked the king as he stepped in stride with the prince.

"Oh, most definitely, you look too sure of yourself, I must take that smirk off your face. So out with it man—do your best! I dare you to find something that would startle me."

Michael's grin grew. Truly, Darien was too easy to bait sometimes. He may be the better swordsman, but his own pride got too much in the way of rational thinking. Hesitating only a moment or two, he went ahead and satisfied his young friend. It was time the man realized he was not invincible—at least not when it came to things of a bone chilling nature. "Ghosts, Darien. You have and will always be decidedly against the visitations of anything of the spiritual, ghouly, phantom, or specter realm—the realm of the dead."

The king watched Darien's face pale as his feet stalled, before continuing, "And no matter how old you or I become, that night of our first haunting will forever ring through my memories. And you boy, would be a fool to deny such aversions." His voice grew low and sinister just to guarantee the prince squirmed. "To deny it, only warrants their return even more…"

## *ABOUT JENNI:*

JENNI JAMES IS the happy mother of seven boisterous children and the author of several book babies that include: Pride & Popularity, Northanger Alibi and Persuaded from The Jane Austen Diaries for teens and Prince Tennyson an inspirational novel. She enjoys writing clean literature for children, teens and adults. Look out for more of her Faerie Tale Collection; Sleeping Beauty and Rumplestiltskin are coming soon! To get all the latest news and updates come find her on facebook: Author Jenni James or visit her website authorjennijames.com she loves to hear from her readers and can be emailed directly at:

jenni@authorjennijames.com

For more StoneHouse Ink titles go to:
http://www.stonehouseink.net

snuggled back down against him.

"You do realize, do you not, that even when I'm angry at you, it is because I care for you? Because this friendship means that much to me, because I need you in my life."

"What would you do without me?" was his hushed reply.

She gasped quietly. "I do not know. I don't want to think about it. The important thing is I have you now and you are more necessary to me than anyone I have ever known."

"And why is that?"

"I don't know." She buried her face in his softness and said, "Perhaps it is because you care. You genuinely care about me and see me differently than anyone ever has before."

"Cecelia," his voice cracked.

"Yes?"

I love you. I love you. I love you. He went to open his mouth repeatedly, but it would not come out. He needed to tell her right then. He needed to share with her his true feelings, so she would understand, and yet, something was preventing him from uttering the words. Was this what the old witch had alluded to before she fell to her death? Was this the warning she had meant to speak of? Or was it something worse?

"Apollo?" She stirred, but did not get up.

"Forgive me; my mind was mulling over a problem just then." When she didn't respond, he continued, "There is something I wish I could tell you, but this enchantment will not let me speak a word of what I wish to you."

"There are certain things you cannot say?"

"Yes."

She turned on her side and buried her hand in his soft coat. "How long have you been an enchanted wolf, your whole life?"

Alexander opened his mouth and realized it was something else he could not speak of. "I am not able to answer that question either."

Her hand pulled free and she lifted her head. "Honestly?" She giggled. "Are you trying to answer and nothing comes out?"

"Precisely."

"Oh, dear, that must be incredibly vexing." And yet she chuckled.

He shook his head and grinned. "You are simply the most sympathetic girl I know."

"I'm sorry!" She smiled. "But you are

quite fascinating, you know."

"I am? I find myself pretty ordinary."

She leaned back against his softness. "Dearest Apollo, you are by far the most intriguing individual I've ever known." Quieting for a moment, she then continued, "So, I wonder what questions I can inquire of you." After thinking for a bit she asked, "Were you always a wolf?"

"No."

Her mouth gaped open. "You were not?"

"No." He sighed and laid his head on his paws.

"Oh, Apollo, I'm terribly sorry." She turned more fully into him and hugged his strong body.

He was certain she would begin to solicit a hundred different questions about what he was before he became a wolf, and how the transformation happened, and who did this to him…all questions he knew he would not be able to answer. But instead, Cecelia surprised him by simply asking—

"Was it difficult to accept this new change?"

He snorted. Was it difficult? Was it

difficult? "Words cannot describe the effect it had me."

"How have you endured it—becoming something you were not?"

"Well—" he inhaled a bit of air and continued, "I had to come to the conclusion that my transformation was needed. Desperately needed. And though it has hurt me and harmed my pride most significantly, it is better that I be the sufferer now, instead of those who would have had failed attempts at life, because of me."

"I do not pretend to understand in the slightest what you are talking of, but if it is in reference to the other night, where you consider yourself a monster, then perhaps it may have been so. But now, my dear, you are anything of the sort  I was not mocking you when I said you are more beautiful than anyone I know of." She moved to sit in front of him, where she could see his reactions.

Alexander's heart began to race on its own accord.

"If you were a monster, if you were cruel in any way at all, I can attest that part of you no longer exists. You have changed.

Referring to your past as you have does indeed
prove it. Treating me as calmly and carefully
and sweetly as you have has proven it as
well. You are generous, you are kind, you
are charitable, and you care—genuinely care
about me—and I am sure countless others as
well. I feel a connection with you I have never
felt with anyone before. I do not understand
all the intricacies of our relationship, but I
promise you, my dear Apollo, I have never
known a man as great as the beast you are."

Her own heart began to triple its speed
as she ascertained the significance of what
she was saying. What her true feelings were
on the subject. It was no accident she was
happier this morning when she had woken.
It was no accident her mood seemed lighter
and at ease with her surroundings. She may
be attracted to the prince, but it was nothing
compared to the feelings this wolf had stirred
in her heart.

Miss Cecelia Hammerstein-Smythe was
most definitely in love.

A blush stole across her features at the
realization, and she was suddenly very grateful
for the darkened sky. It was then she felt that

perhaps she had spoken long enough. She needed to be alone, to fully embrace and understand what she now knew to be true, to sort through the emotions cascading about her.

She leaned down and placed a kiss upon his nose and another on his brow, before standing and stating, "Forgive me, but I must go now."

Alexander sat up as well. "Cecelia?"

She waved her hand in an attempt to brush aside the obvious abrupt nature of her departure. "It's the time—I did not realize how long I had already been here." In great nervousness and haste, she dipped a curtsy and crossed the stream.

"Cecelia, wait."

She turned to look back, the moonbeams streaming all around. "Yes?"

"Thank you." His eyes pleaded with hers to understand all he could not say.

She smiled a short smile and said, "You are most welcome." And then on a whim and before she lost her courage, she rushed out the words, "I love you. I don't care what you look like. I do not love the prince, I cannot love him, because I am in love with you," before fleeing up the hill and out of sight.

Prince Alexander's jaw dropped and he would have rushed after her in that moment to stay with her longer, but the transformation began before he had a chance to explain a thing.

She had broken the spell.

He was now forever the prince.

The one she did not trust, the one she did not love.

"Oh? And how shall you think of me?"

Cecelia grinned and curtsied deeply before him. "My dear Apollo, with your great wisdom and supreme charm, I'm sure you are nothing less than a King in my eyes." She bounced back up. "I will always think of you as the grandest friend I have ever had."

"Just don't go spilling your secrets, or you'll spill my blood."

"Precisely!" she answered with a chortle, and then, "Goodbye!" she called, her feet carrying her down the path back home.

Alexander watched her go until he could not see her anymore, until not even the sound of her boots hitting the dirt or the swish of her skirts made it to his ears. And then he whispered quietly to the glistening brook, "You are already flying, my wingless bird, and you do not even know it."

The wolf smiled and hesitantly stood, shaking free the fatigue that had come across his form. There were a few more hours of moonlight left and he had yet to determine whether Prince Alexander would indeed show up on the morrow at the Hammerstein-Smythe house or not. He was just settling himself into

# Chapter Twelve

"CECELIA," THE BEAST called out as she crossed the brook.

She turned, marveling at the way the moonbeams streamed all around him. He really did seem enchanted. "Yes?"

"I have seen you for two days in a row; will I see you for a third as well?"

She laughed. "I do not perceive how you could ever keep me away now." Holding the necklace up she explained, "This, in a manner, bonds us, don't you think?"

"Indubitably."

"Good. Then I shall wear it at all times and think of you."